AF498077

GLÒRIA ARIMON

TALES FROM BAGHDAD

"Ursa Maior" Collection

Tales from Baghdad
First edition 2010
Original title: *Contes de Bagdad*

English translation: Eva Cañada
Arabic translation: Fadi Hadeeb
Inside illustration: Helena Ruiz
Cover photograph: Glòria Arimon

Publisher: Marge Books –València 558, àtic 2.ª – 08026 Barcelona, Spain
www.marge.es – Tel. +34-932 449 130 – Fax +34-932 310 865

Publishing director: David Soler
Managing editors: Hèctor Soler, Laura Matos, Anna Palacios
Editing: Sandra Martínez
Editorial contributor: Leanne Fairley
Editorial production: Miquel Àngel Roig
Mark-up editor: Mercedes Lara
Printed by: Més Gran Seveis Gràfics i Digitals (Santa Coloma
de Cervelló, Barcelona)

ISBN: 978-84-92442-90-4
Dipòsit Legal: B-

GLÒRIA ARIMON
with the collaboration of Josep Lorman

TALES FROM BAGHDAD

This publication is part of the Education for Peace Project of:

COMPROMESOS
amb el mòn

Produced with the support from:

Committed to the world (Compromesos amb el món) are a small non-governmental organization (NGO), founded in 2007 in Catalonia. We promote and support international cooperation projects. Peace education is one of our principal goals. We have created this book for all the organisations who work for the same aim.

Information and contact: www.compromesos.cat.

Note

Please, see **www.marge.es** for proposals designed for anyone who wishes to work on the problems experienced in Irak and to debate about the customs, traditions and values for Education for Peace.

INDEX

The waves of the Tigris have been chained up
How are we supposed to dream of travels from now on?
What island will we go to?

Sargon Bulus (Iraqi poet)

INTRODUCTION

THE stories that we present you in this book are focused on three characters from *One Thousand and One Nights*.

The stories included in *One Thousand and One Nights* have very different origins. The oldest stories come from India; there is another group of Persian tales; a third group includes Islamic stories that take place in Iraq, and finally there is a fourth group of stories set in Egypt. There is proof written in Arabic that goes back to the ninth century. On 1704, Galland, the French archeologist and expert on Eastern affairs, published the first translated volume of the work, enabling it to reach the European public, with remarkable success. As a result, in the nineteenth century new stories were added, like *Sinbad the Sailor* and, later on, some tales that had been circulating separately, like *Ali Baba and the Forty Thieves* and *Aladdin and the Magic Lamp*.

The story of *One Thousand and One Nights* begins when the sovereign of Baghdad, the cruel King Shahryar, finds out that his wife is cheating on him with another man. Enraged, he decides that he will bring a different virgin and girl of noble blood to his bed every night and, when the sun comes out, he will kill her. The central character of the story is Scheherazade, the daughter of a vizier, and plans to put an end to this slaughter of young women. She volunteers to meet the king, and every night she tells him a different tale that she leaves unfinished before the day comes. Thus, the king does not kill her, since he wants to know how the story ends and has to wait until night falls. The tales deal with very different subjects: love, fantasy, intrigue, knighthood and adventure.

The tales about *Sinbad, Ali Baba* and *Aladdin* were added to the initial stories, and we have situated them in the present-day Iraq because the land belonging to this country corresponds, at least partly, to ancient Mesopotamia, between the Tigris and Euphrates rivers that flow into the Persian

Gulf. Over 5,500 years ago, one of the first forms of writing was invented in that territory. In 1990, the first facilities bombed by North American and British troops in their attack on Iraq were the paper mills, and the United Nations forbade them to import spare parts related to graphic arts and printing industries. At the same time, they forbade the use of pencils under the pretence that the graphite they contained could be used as military material.

Throughout history, boys and girls from around the world have lived adventures and love affairs in places very different from where we live. All of them had in common the desire to learn, to play, to have a good time, to love... For many years the lives of the young boys and girls in Iraq have not been able to be like ours, because of the many wars, first provoked by the dictator and then by the US occupation. Hundreds of thousands of people died during the first years of the occupation, one-third of whom were of a young age. One out of every eight inhabitants has been forced to flee their home or the country itself. Baghdad, the capital, has no shore. So, in order to reach the sea it is necessary to cross Basra, the city located to the south, after the confluence of the Tigris and Euphrates rivers. In that city, before the occupation, there was a sculpture of Sinbad gazing upon the sea. In Baghdad, there were a series of sculptures representing Ali Baba and the thieves in a large public square. The past of their legendary characters is present all over the country.

On 2002, in Basra, I met two kids who worked as shoeshine boys. They worked during the mornings and in the afternoon they went to school. They told me they were happy. From a distance, I have often remembered them as well as the landscapes from Iraq: the desert, the marshes, the shores, the ruins of ancient civilizations... And, most of all, the look in the eyes of the boys and girls I met on the streets. All of them wanted to be happy, like the characters in the tales written centuries back. And since I cannot and do not want to forget, one day I closed my eyes and started to imagine the heroes of old, Sinbad, Ali Baba and Aladdin, with the faces, clothes and troubles of the young boys and girls who live in present-day Iraq. That is where these tales came from: they have the looks of the shoeshine boys, and of the little children that played in the yard at the mosque, studied at the school or lay in the hospital beds.

The stories of *One Thousand and One Nights* represent the triumph of art and culture over barbarism, because eventually the king, after so many nights listening to those stories, spares Scheherazade's life. Reality is changed by words. We'd like these *Tales from Baghdad* to also help us understand that words and reason are the only weapons we need to use in the case of a confrontation. We can see what is currently happening in Iraq almost live on television, with the risk of getting used to other people's grief and becoming immune to suffering and death. We hope that, by reading these stories, fantasy will help us recover the truth. Both young people and adults can make things change. It's all up to us.

Glòria Arimon

SINBAD

THE place where the Tigris and Euphrates rivers were located was so beautiful that some say that's where Earthly Paradise once was. Water flowed everywhere, in the shape of rivers, channels and ponds. In between there were all kinds of fruit trees: apricot trees, orange trees, apple trees, pear trees. And, above all, there were long-trunked palm trees from the tops of which hung bunches of fat, sweet dates. There was also a large amount of livestock: poultry, horses, donkeys, goats, lambs, cats, bats. A small village called Al Qura was located at the point where both rivers met. The Shatt-al-Arab river originated there, and some hundreds of miles to the south it flowed into the Persian Gulf. This deep river allowed big boats to reach the village from the sea.

In the year 637, among water channels and palm trees, a caliph founded a town that, in no time at all, came to have thousands of inhabitants: Basra. The sea was close at hand just down the river, so they built a port, Um Qasar, where fishing and mainly sailing boats were moored. In a few years, those men arrived in China. They sailed beyond the confines they could see, discovered new horizons, different worlds, colors, flavors, looks, languages and loves.

Many centuries after that, a boy lived in Basra. He was tall and tanned, his eyes were big and round and his hair was black and curly. His name was Sinbad. Hamid, his uncle, dry and wrinkled by the years, had taken him in when his mother died giving birth to her second child. His father had died just a few months before due to very high fever, which turned the healthy, strong man into a bundle of flesh and bones in no time at all.

Sinbad spent his day on the street, at first playing with other kids, and soon enough trying to make a living so he could have something to eat. Very often he went to the bank of the river and, from there, he took a glimpse of the little islets set in the middle of the water and watched the merchant traffic. More and more boats were coming

*The first years he sailed in a barge
just as a helper.*

from abroad, some of them from very far away, with men from different races and with products they didn't have there.

One day, just after his thirteenth birthday, he was looking at the men who disembarked from the arriving ships and he made up his mind: "I'm going to be a sailor." And so it was. His uncle had died and he wasn't responsible for looking after him anymore.

The first years he sailed in a barge just as a helper. But after a while he saved enough money to buy his own boat and become his own master. In the middle of the sea, he watched the seagulls fly. In the wintertime, he let the sun caress his face and arms. In the summertime, when it was too hot, he took shelter under an awning. In the middle of the sea, he was happy. He felt alone and in company at the same time. He set the bait and waited until the fish bit it. It didn't matter whether it took them one hour or two. Time had stopped.

Sinbad was a very restless young man, and soon he felt that going out fishing every day was too easy and boring. He couldn't stop staring at the horizon, and by the evening, when he arrived at his hut, he counted the money he had saved from selling fish. Every night he thought of how many years it would take him to save enough money to buy a good boat to travel further into the sea. Most of the boys of his age, who lived within a family, were waiting for their parents to choose a girl for them to marry. But he was in no hurry. Of course he liked girls, but... it was something he'd worry about later on. It seemed to him that, for the time being, there were more important things to do.

One pleasant and quiet night he went to the street. The moon, full and round, reflected on the canal that streamed before his house. When he looked at it, it seemed to him that the moon was winking at him. Sinbad loved everything that surrounded him. He felt it very deep in his heart: that landscape, his friends, the river, the old market in Kawit, the busy Al-Wasan Street, the minarets of the more than thirty mosques in town, the bridges above the canals, the many pastry shops. But he needed a change. With this in mind, he entered the coffeehouse to have a tea and a hookah and meet some friends. As usual, there were only men in the shop. It was not common to see women in there. An old man was saying that he was too old to keep sailing the seas, and wanted to retire. Sinbad knew that this man's boat was good and big, so he made an offer to buy it. He'd give a down payment at the beginning and he'd pay the rest of the money over the next few years. After discussing and bargaining about the price for a while, they came to an agreement, the way honest men did. No document was needed: their word was enough.

A few days later, equipped with a container full of water and a bag loaded with food, Sinbad set sail. It was his first journey towards adventure. A soft wind was blowing while he looked at the town that was growing smaller as he sailed away. Right at the point where the river reached the sea after crossing the big delta, once he passed the island that he had gone round so many times and that he knew it by heart, Sinbad steered to the east and let the boat lead him. Since the wind was not too strong, the ship sailed slowly... until the sea became completely flat. There was no wind, so he drifted to a stop. Sinbad was not afraid: he used those moments of quietness to sleep or have something to eat. The problem, though, appeared when the headwind blew, because it dragged him in the opposite direction to where he wanted to go. So, three days after he had set sail, he was again at the mouth of the river. He then realized that his determination was not enough, and that he needed to acquire some knowledge from people who had been sailing the sea for many years.

He asked some experienced sailors many things, and, even though he could not read or write, he could draw some rough maps. Once he did that, he gathered some supplies, took a little box with the jewels he had inherited from his family, as well as various items and products to sell. With his load, he left the port again. This time, and following the advice given by the experienced sailors, he didn't stray too far from the shore and headed for the Persian coasts. The trip went well, the wind was favorable and, after a few days, he came upon an unknown city, where he found people who spoke another language. A man he met at the harbor told him that, depending on the place they came from, people spoke so differently that they could not even understand each other. However, people used to sailing through different countries managed to understand others and make others understand them.

"The most important thing," said the man, "is wanting to communicate."

During the days he stayed there, Sinbad sold the dates and the salt he had transported, and then a merchant in the marketplace bought the necklaces, the two rings and the bracelet that had been his family treasures. With the money he got, he purchased silk fabrics and products that they didn't have in his home country. When he returned to Basra, he sold everything and earned a pouch of money that he used to pay part of his debt and to buy some more goods he could sell. For a year, Sinbad went to and from the Persian ports as many times as he could, purchasing and selling goods. Every time he went a little further. He already knew the Persian shore by heart, first green and lavish, and then very dry. He had been told that, when you left the Strait of Hormuz behind, the sea opened wide and became huge. From there he could reach India and China. He had also sailed along the western shore of the Arabian Peninsula, but he had never gone beyond the Qatar Peninsula because of the very strong and dangerous currents. At that time, ferocious pirates attacked every vessel that sailed that part of the sea. That's why it was called the Pirate Coast.

After not too long, Sinbad had already paid off his debt to the old man that had sold him his boat, so he decided to hire a helper. His name was Beb Radin.

For a year, Sinbad went to and from the Persian ports as many times as he could, purchasing and selling goods.

With all his travels, Sinbad learned lots he hadn't learned before. He met people to admire, and also people to fear, and he had to face many dangers: storms, thieves, swindlers. But he was a very clever boy. Even though he was illiterate, he had managed to understand the languages people spoke wherever he went. He had a good ear and a fast mouth, but he knew when to keep it shut, and he certainly knew how to keep a secret. He had a friend in each port, a girl that looked at him in silence in each town. Every time he returned to Basra, the place he could call home even though he never stayed for long, he felt his body quiver. When he saw the silhouette of the mosques, which he knew like his own shadow, he always cried:

"I'm safe! I'm home!"

Sinbad still remembered some stories his uncle had told him about the time when Genghis Khan, Emperor of Mongolia, arrived to these lands. All he left behind were traces of horror and destruction, unlike other people such as the Abbasids, the Assyrians or the Greeks, who brought culture and wealth. He had been told that his current country was once occupied by the Ottoman Empire. Then the tribes united to face a common enemy, the British Empire, which occupied that land and wanted to become the master. When they left, it was not easy for them to start walking, for every land made its own war.

While he was sailing, Sinbad had lots of time to think. He always wondered why men couldn't live in peace: fishing, farming, trading … and loving. Sometimes when he talked about that in a coffeehouse, the older men laughed at him.

"When you grow older you'll see. It's every man for himself, especially those in command. There are some who have a lot of money, and the rest of us have just enough to get by."

Sinbad then kept silent, but he had a hope that someday he would find a treasure hidden on one of those little islands in the Gulf. When he dared to confess this thought to anyone, they told him:

"The greatest treasure we have here is crude oil. But it doesn't belong to us either."

They dug very deep into the land, as far as its soul, where they found the black gold. Sinbad used oil to set the fire, to cook, to sail, but they told him that, the way the world was going, it had many other uses. Not in his country, because it was not developed enough, but in America, on the other side of the vast ocean, it was used to make almost everything, from window blinds to buckets.

An ocean, Sinbad thought, an ocean is a never ending sea, where it takes weeks and weeks to reach a shore and where there are such huge tempests that a boat like mine wouldn't last a day. America... Will I ever be able to get there? The eternal dream. In America, people were rich, they owned boats and cars, they lived in nice, clean houses, they wore good clothes, every child went to school. He was now eighteen years old, and at that time the children in his country went to school and could go to see the doctor when they were ill. But the powerful people and those in command were so far away! Not long ago, Baghdad was thirty hours away by car. One bad day, he heard in a coffeehouse that his country was at war with the neighboring nation, the Persians, a land that was known as Iran. The conflict came from afar. They had always been fighting for the possession of the river and Khuzestan Province, where there was plenty of oil.

"Why?" he asked those men who were drinking tea and smoking hookahs.

Everyone looked at him and shrugged their shoulders. One man answered, "We, the common people, never know why our rulers participate in wars. And, eventually, it's always us who get harmed, whether those wars are won or lost."

And so it was. Sinbad didn't dare to sail to the Persian shore anymore. Instead, he went to the west, but he didn't feel at ease there either. Very often he saw and heard big birds of fire flying through the skies and spitting out flames and smoke. Those were very tough years, because the bombs reached Basra. Eight infernal years. During that time, no family in town remained untouched: fathers and sons of age were called up to fight against their neighbors; mothers and children were bombed and brutally killed in their own homes. Even the fish seemed to be hiding, they were so hard to catch! That war didn't have a winner and a loser: it ended up even, with a million dead between the two sides. The outlines of the sunken ships that remained in the harbor were a reminder of the destruction. Then, in honor of all the dead generals, the president of his country ordered the building, on the seafront of Basra, of 250 statues representing each one of the generals that had died in the battles against Iran, with their right arms pointing away to the other side of the shore, their gazes like ice, their rifles on their backs, still challenging their enemy.

But human beings have an amazing capacity to react and survive. The inhabitants of Basra rebuilt their city, re-erected their mosques, reopened their stores, reconstructed the bridges over the channels, the marketplace became a bustle of colors and movement again, and the fishermen and merchants returned to the sea.

Sinbad sailed again, and with the support of Beb Radin, his young helper, he sold goods that he brought from Basra and bought more abroad, which he sold back in his own town. Time had gone by and he still hadn't got married.

"You must make sure not to wait too long," his friends told him affectionately.

They advised him to get married, which he eventually did to a young girl, who was an orphan like him and who lived with her aunt and her cousin. Zainab was sixteen, and his father and her two brothers had been killed at war. According to tradition, Sinbad presented his request for matrimony to the head of the family, the girl's cousin, who it was not too hard to convince: they were poor, and if she got married there would be one mouth less to feed. So, Sinbad bought a house in the district of Zahra. It was a good moment to do so because there were

*Sinbad told Zainab that he wanted to set sail
for a few days so that he could share with
her his greatest treasure, the ocean.*

many people in need who were selling their homes at low prices because of the war. But before moving in to their new home, Sinbad told Zainab that he wanted to set sail for a few days so that he could share with her his greatest treasure, the ocean.

"I want you to love it the way I do," he told her.

This time they went all alone, without the helper. The first day, Sinbad started to look at her with tenderness. What he liked the most about her were her honey-colored, round eyes and her soft and gentle skin. They would have children, for sure. He would make them go to school and he would teach them to sail the seas, he thought, as he stared toward the horizon. They hardly knew each other, and the girl looked at him suspiciously. Perhaps she was worrying because she didn't know what kind of man she had married. Zainab had studied at school, and so she could read and write, and she could also cook. The first few quiet nights, with a full moon in the sky, lying on the boat deck, they held each other's hands and shared the secrets of their childhood. Some days later they began to discover the mysteries of their bodies, and finally, under a roof of palm trees on a Persian beach, they became lovers. Three weeks later, when they came back to Basra, they were no longer the same. She felt happy and fearless, eager to hear more about all the things Sinbad knew and also eager to teach him how to write, just as they had agreed. He, whose long-time lover was the sea, was feeling doubly in love with life now that he had his wife by his side. He didn't ask for more.

A year after their marriage they had their first child, a boy they named Ali. Sinbad never thought that being a parent would bring him so much joy. At that time he didn't undertake long trips, he tried to be back home as early as possible, and when he was not trading, he went fishing. But his happiness didn't last long. Not much later, the president of his country started another war and invaded the neighboring region of Kuwait. The occupation didn't last more than a few days because a group of countries, led by the United States and Great Britain, made him turn back. Those were days of grief and death. Basra, just like many other cities, was bombed through and through with depleted uranium bombs. There was no place to hide. The huge forests of palm trees that covered the banks of the Shatt-al-Arab river were severely damaged, and all the tree tops had been clipped off. The whole shore was barren and naked. Some weeks later, the attacks stopped, but what came next was another kind of war. It was the war of suffering, the war of not having anything to eat, the war of the fear of planes flying over the city. It was the aftermath of the embargo.

Meanwhile, Zainab was pregnant again, and she did not feel well. Sinbad hardly dared to leave the house, but he needed to look for a job, any job, to feed his family. When the time came for the child to be born, they went to hospital because they felt that something wasn't right. A girl was born there, Latifa, who the doctors diagnosed with leukemia. They explained that, from the war on, many children had been born with malformations and other illnesses. The newborn seemed like a little bird that could be knocked down by a simple gust of wind. Once they were back home, Sinbad spent most of his time by his wife's side. She felt very weak, but nonetheless tried to breast-feed and take care of Latifa.

One day, when Sinbad came back from running some errands, he found his wife very pale and weak. Cholera, the disease she suffered from since her pregnancy, had progressed until it damaged her

*One day, when Sinbad came back from
running some errands, he found his wife
very pale and weak.*

whole body. She died like a little bird, and Sinbad felt lonelier than ever. After her burial, sitting on the bank of the river, he kept embracing Ali until it was dark. He didn't know what to do or where to go. He needed to work to feed his two children, but who could take care of them? He left them for a few days with a neighbor, but she herself recommended that he marry again, because he needed a woman to take care of the kids. Sinbad didn't feel like getting married again, but that woman took it upon herself to find a girl of his age who was widowed when her husband was killed during the war. She had two children, one of them was two years old and the other just a few months, and she went to live in Sinbad's house. So she could breast-feed Latifa and he could go out fishing or exchange some of the products they got with their ration card for others they needed more. They couldn't even drink clean water, since it was polluted with uranium, while the farmers complained because their fields were barren, just like themselves. There were no more dates on the palm trees, nor figs on the fig trees. This was their punishment for their president's misdeeds. Sinbad wished that nobody had ever discovered oil in their country, because that way they would have been left alone!

Little Latifa, so fragile and tender, couldn't bear her illness and also died. A teardrop slipped down Sinbad's cheek; he had grown very old in a very short time. The muezzin called for prayer from the minaret of the Imam Ali mosque. Sinbad raised his head and looked into the sky. Ten years had passed since that war. In the meantime, Sinbad got used to his new wife's company, and vice versa. His only aim was to get food for his family. He had left behind his happy days, when he sailed the seas, free, buying and selling, feeling fear at times, but always open to all the possibilities life offered him. He often thought of Zainab, who had died without seeing Ali grow up. The same Ali he had promised he'd teach to sail, still had a huge capacity for happiness playing with other kids in the muddy street, in the middle of the broken sewers, or at the cold and sad school. Ali, his future. It seemed as though nothing else could happen, but the Americans had been long threatening a new war. Many people couldn't believe it, but one day when Sinbad had taken his boat to go fishing, he heard the sound of airplanes. He raised his head and saw it was not like usual. This time there were many planes, and they were much bigger. He immediately thought of his wife and kids, who were at home. He started the motor of the boat and quickly returned to town, but he couldn't reach the port. It was filled with hundreds of boats and occupied by British soldiers, who were everywhere. He had to turn around and anchor somewhere nearby, and from there, he had to go on foot. At the seafront, the Sheraton Hotel was surrounded by combat cars, and groups of desperate people were going inside and taking everything they could before the passiveness of the soldiers. In little time, the concrete giant that had been the symbol of Iraqi luxury became a heap of ruins.

When he finally reached his district, Sinbad saw a crowd of people. He didn't know what was going on until he could force his way through the mob: his own home and other houses in the neighborhood had been entirely wrecked by a missile. He let go a heartbreaking cry and started running towards it. He could get in through a window, and breaking through the debris, he found the bodies of his wife and children, all of them dead. Next to his wife, Ali's body was still breathing. He reached out to him in tears and held him. He felt the little boy's last breath. He took him in his arms and went out to the street. He noticed that the crowd had suddenly hushed. A row of tanks approached. People began to hide and Sinbad was left alone with his son in his arms. He began to walk toward the tanks that were forming a circle in a nearby esplanade. He carried Ali's body, a body covered in blood, the body of his beloved son, who was to sail the Arabian seas, discover new countries and new people, learn languages, live adventures, love and laugh... He walked towards the tanks holding his son, getting closer and closer to them. He couldn't see or hear anything. He had no more tears. Suddenly, the tanks stopped. Some journalists arrived in a car and shouted to the soldiers:

"Do not touch him, can't you see he is carrying his dead son?" Then they began to take pictures with their cameras.

That photograph travelled the world. So Sinbad became known all over, and a humanitarian organization invited him to go to America and explain what had happened to him. But he, who years before had dreamed of crossing the ocean, declined the invitation. A journalist tried to convince him:

"If you go there, you'll be on television and in the newspapers, you'll be able to tell your story. You'll be able to say whatever you want. You'll become famous and perhaps you'll have the chance to stay there. You have no future here."

But he couldn't see or hear a thing. His future had just died in his arms.

America existed. He had heard about it long ago, so he knew it existed. You don't need to go somewhere to believe that a place exists. Now he had very strong proof: America had taken his wife, his daughter, his son, his second wife and her children. It had taken his friends and neighbors, it had poisoned the lettuce and tomatoes in their gardens. America existed since years ago it had attacked them and the people in the villages and in the countryside. And then it promoted an embargo during which five thousand children under five died every month. He already knew America existed, he had been given enough evidence. He didn't want to go there.

"I belong here. I belong to the town where I was born and raised, where I've been so happy, where I found love. This is my home, all blown up, polluted and full of smoke, but it is my home. I have nothing left: no boat, no house, no family,

He walked towards the tanks holding his son,
getting closer and closer to them.

no hope. I don't even have teardrops left, but I'm still a person."

Sinbad didn't have guns, or missiles, or bombs, or rifles, or – of course – combat cars, but he had two hands and two legs, and a brain to think. Sitting in front of those waters he had loved so much, he decided that nobody would step on his dignity. He stood on his feet. He was holding a stone in his hand, inside his pocket. He walked with determination, feeling no fear. A stone from the beach, round, shaped by the sea, and he was holding it firmly. Basra was his home and nobody was going to cast him out. That stone gave him strength as he caressed it: it represented his sea, his town, his music and his mosques. It represented the people he had loved the most. He was walking faster and faster, not noticing the thunder and lightning of war. When he arrived in the centre of Basra, it seemed as though he suddenly woke up: he turned his head and saw many other men, women and children holding, like him, a stone in their hand. They walked together, without saying a word, with determination, with their heads raised to the sky. They were growing in number, and they were feeling strong. They had what it took to win: they were right. It could take them some time, but they were going to win. One day, they would be back in the sea, and they'd be happy again.

The Iraqi people have already won.
That's why their children's arms are ripped off:
if they have already won, at least they won't
be able to give the victory sign with their fingers.

Santiago Alba Rico

ALI BABA

A LI Baba had married a poor girl, Morgana, and they always had found it difficult to make ends meet. Ali went to the forest to collect wood and pick asparagus; he also collected dates from the palm trees and chestnuts when it was the right time of year, and sold them all at the marketplace. His brother Kassim, on the other hand, married a rich girl. He was a merchant and had a natural ability to make money grow. He bought goods at one price and sold them for much more money: he didn't have many scruples. He bought his products smuggling them from the bordering countries —food, machinery, oil, medicines— and he distributed them through a network of dealers. His only emblem was money. The American occupation made his business decrease, but all in all he got along very well, selling products to both the occupants and the resistance.

One day, when Ali Baba was in the forest, he saw a group of off-road vehicles that raised heavy clouds of dust as they approached. He was afraid, so he went to hide inside a nearby cave. If those vehicles were driven by the Americans and they found him there, even doing something as normal as chopping wood, they might arrest him. From a dark corner of the cave, holding his breath so as not to be discovered, he could see how the soldiers, who were indeed American, took boxes full of weapons out of the vehicles and hid them in a covered deposit in the very cave he was hiding in. At first he was puzzled, but then he thought it was a reserve deposit to keep weapons safe should the resistance attack their quarters and destroy the weapon stores. Those Americans were very clever.

Once they placed all the boxes inside, one of the soldiers entered a code in a keyboard hidden on the wall of the cave, and the door closed the same way it had opened. Then, the soldier put the piece of paper where the code was written inside his pocket. He was the last one left inside the cave. However, before he left, he took his handker-

…he could see how the soldiers, who were indeed American, took boxes full of weapons out of the vehicles and hid them in a covered deposit in the very cave he was hiding in.

chief out of his pocket to wipe the perspiration from his face. After he dried his face, he kept the handkerchief and left the cave without noticing that the paper with the code on it had fallen out of his pocket. Ali Baba, who kept his eyes on the soldier all this time, didn't leave his hiding place until he heard the car engines going away, and then he went straight to the piece of paper. He picked it up and examined it. It was a combination of ten numbers and letters that he shyly typed into the keyboard on the wall, just as he had seen the soldier do. The door opened, and before his astonished eyes dozens of stacked boxes full of weapons appeared.

"For the sake of Allah! This is a real arsenal!" he whispered.

And he immediately thought of taking some weapons to defend his family. In his district, it was very common to see squads of soldiers bursting into the houses by surprise, turning everything upside down and taking away all family members. They said they were looking for terrorists. Very few people came back and if they did, they were in such a bad state that they would be better off dead. At least that's what people thought.

On the other hand, having a weapon at home was a very dangerous thing... He didn't know what to do, but eventually the desire to look after his family was stronger and he took a semiautomatic rifle and a handful of magazines. Then, he entered the code again to close the door and he went home.

Ali Baba was very excited about his discovery and told his wife about it. They decided to hide the weapon in a secret place in the house that would at the same time be easy to reach should the soldiers take them by surprise in the middle of the night. As they were talking, they didn't notice that Ahmed, their youngest child, was in the next room listening to what they said.

The next day, Ahmed, who went every afternoon to his uncle Kassim's house to play with his cousin, said:

"Nothing can happen to us from now on, uncle Kassim. My father found a very good weapon in a cave. And if the soldiers come during the night to harm us, we will kill them!"

When Kassim heard that, he opened his eyes wide as a pair of oranges. Weapons were always a good business! He had to know where his brother had found his.

That same evening, Kassim went to see Ali Baba and asked him about the weapon and how he had obtained it. Ali Baba told him about his discovery.

Then, Kassim, motivated by greed, suggested that his brother take all the weapons and sell them to the best buyer, inside or outside the country.

"We could get a fortune if we sold the weapons in Afghanistan," he said enthusiastically.

"Are you mad? What you propose is very dangerous. What do you think the Americans will do when they see that the cave is empty?"

"When they realize that, we'll both be rich and far away from here."

The two brothers argued for a long time, until Kassim threatened Ali Baba to the Americans if he didn't accept his wish to do business with the weapons. Ali Baba thought that his brother loved him less than he loved money, as he had already proven on many an occasion. How could there be such mean people in the world? They both were born of the same mother, they had drunk the same milk and gone to the same school. How could they be so different?

"Can't you see that if I let you do this, we'll put not only ourselves in danger, but our families as well? Don't you care about your family?" Ali Baba said.

Kassim, furious with his brother's stubbornness, approached him and seized him by the neck.

*A body inside a coffin. A hole at the cemetery
with the head pointing to Mecca.
Teardrops and crying.*

"I have the chance to do the biggest business deal of my life and you won't stop me. You'd better tell me where the cave is, or I swear I'll go straight to the American quarters as soon as I leave this house."

A chill ran up Ali Baba's spine. His brother was surely capable of anything, and much more. So he told him where the deposit was and gave him the paper with the code to get in and out. "Do as you like," Ali Baba thought, but he didn't want to have anything else to do with him or the weapons.

Next morning, Kassim took his van and went to the cave. He impatiently typed in the secret code, the door opened and he entered the weapons store. He didn't want to be seen while he examined the place, so he typed the code again on the inside keypad and the door closed. By the beard of the Prophet! When he saw everything that that pile of boxes contained, he got very excited. If he sold it all on the black market, he could make a fortune! It was his chance to become rich forever. And once he sold everything, he'd take his family and move to another country. Let the Americans look for him then. He was fed up with so many years of suffering and war. They would go to some place where a businessman like him was well considered and had chances to prosper. An emerging country. China, for example. There were so many possibilities in the world!

Without wasting a second, Kassim separated a few boxes and left them near the door in order to load them into the van. When the moment came to leave the cave, he put his hand into his pocket and looked for the paper with the code. But he couldn't find it!

"Where did I put the piece of paper?" he whispered nervously as he turned all of his pockets inside out. "I must have dropped it on the ground while I was moving the boxes. Let's see... calm down... I have to find it."

He examined the floor inch by inch, but he still couldn't find the paper. He spent a good while searching, until he desperately started to try out different codes that seemed familiar to him: DX450MA789. Nothing. DZ450MA739. Nothing! JX450ME789. Nothing!! The door wouldn't open. He was getting more and more anxious. Fat as he was, he sweated like a pig whose neck was about to be slashed. "I'll find it, I'll find it," he kept on saying to cheer himself up. But no, the right combination didn't come out. His head spun and he heard a dazing buzz. He eventually realized that the buzz was not only inside his head, but there was a humming coming from the outside, a humming like the one made by an engine. Yes, it was the sound of car engines approaching... and then stopping!

Kassim remembered, in a whirl of thoughts inspired by fear, the warnings his brother gave him. And he just had time to hide behind some boxes as he complained about his ambition. All his precautions were useless, though, because the soldiers had seen his van outside and it didn't take them more than five minutes to find him.

Meanwhile, at home, his wife Fatima started to worry when Kassim didn't come back. She knew what he had gone to do, and as time passed, her anguish grew stronger and stronger. She finally appealed to Ali Baba. When it grew dark, Ali Baba went to the cave and discovered, right at the entrance, his brother's body turned into a pile of bloody flesh that some wild dog had already started to eat away. The van wasn't there. He picked him up and secretly turned back home with the dead body. What was he supposed to do now?

"I didn't dare to bury him right there because I was afraid the soldiers would come back," he told his wife. "On the other hand, I can't take him to his house because Fatima would start to cry and she would attract the neighbors' attention. What can we do?"

Morgana, who was very clever, as well as beautiful, immediately a solution. She suggested leaving Kassim's body hidden inside a bag in the yard, under a stack of old furniture. It was wintertime, and the body would remain in good condition for a while. Once they did that, she told Ali Baba to go to the police and report the theft of his brother's van.

"If they ask you why your brother didn't come himself to report the theft, tell them he is very ill."

The very next day, early in the morning, Morgana went to the chemist's. She said:

"Can you give me a remedy for my brother-in-law, Kassim, who is feeling very sick? We had to take him to our house because his wife can't take care of him by herself."

The chemist gave her some medicines for the stomach pain, just as the woman had described to him, and they let a day go by. The next day, she went back to the chemist's saying that her brother-in-law was feeling worse. The third day she said he had died and nobody was surprised. Death was very ordinary since the invasion began. They had not allowed their sister-in-law to go out to the street in all this time, because they didn't want the hoax to be discovered. Then, Kassim's family announced the burial, and everybody found it very normal. A body inside a coffin. A hole at the cemetery with the head pointing to Mecca. Teardrops and crying. The sympathy of friends and neighbors. Some sweets and pastries to say thank you.

The problem of getting rid of Kassim's body was solved. But there was one more problem left. The Americans were very intrigued and wanted to know who the man was that they had caught unawares inside the cave. As sometimes happens, the soldiers had shot first and then asked questions. And since the shots had been very accurate, the intruder couldn't answer any of the questions they wanted to ask him. Who was he? How did he enter the cave? Had someone given him the code? And if so, who else knew it and who were they?

As a precaution, the Americans took the weapons away from the cave and hid them elsewhere. Then, they started to investigate about the van. Thanks to the administrative chaos of Baghdad, it took them a week to find out that the van was owned by a merchant called Kassim, who had been buried three days ago due to a severe illness.

*The group left the police station,
crossed a good part of town and arrived
at the door of Ali Baba's house.*

"If he was so ill, what was his van doing in front of the cave?" Inspector Fahad, of the Iraqi police, asked Ali Baba.

"His van had just been stolen that same afternoon," Ali Baba answered, as calmly as he could and he showed them warrant for the theft report.

There was nothing to say. But the Inspector was not fully convinced and he found it all very shady. And that's exactly what he told the Americans. They didn't have any evidence that Ali Baba knew about the cave, and they knew that he didn't take any part in his brother's business. But he was a suspect, and they didn't want to take any risks. Ali Baba and his family had to be arrested and interrogated. But since Ali Baba was a very popular and loved figure in his neighborhood, and his arrest might cause some kind of trouble, Inspector Fahad suggested taking them away secretly and without causing a stir. So he devised a plan that seemed taken right from a tale in *One Thousand and One Nights.*

"There's a huge oil trade in this place, is that correct? And you have seen that merchants, due to the problems they find in getting gasoline, have returned to the old system of using donkeys to transport their goods, right?" Inspector Fahad, who wanted to gain some credit in front of the Americans, said. "So, my men and I will become oil merchants and will bring Ali Baba, his wife and his four children to your quarters without being noticed."

The Americans laughed at Fahad's idea, but they accepted it. If he did as he said, Fahad would have a supply of chocolate for as long as they were there. And Fahad felt a real passion for chocolate!

Inspector Fahad bought eight vessels and loaded them on four donkeys, pretending they were full of oil. But only the first two vessels were actually full of oil. The rest of them had a policeman inside. The group left the police station, crossed a good part of town and arrived at the door of Ali Baba's house. The sun had set among the mountains and it was starting to be very cold. Inspector Fahad, dressed as an oil merchant, knocked on the door and told Ali Baba he was an old friend of his brother Kassim. He had gone to his house, but before he could knock on the door, some neighbors told him that Kassim had died and that his family was very upset. That's why he was asking him for lodgings that night. He didn't want to bother the dead man's family. It was late now, and the next day he had to continue his way to Kazimiyah to sell his oil.

"I don't trust the police, you know?" Fahad said very convincingly. "If I leave the donkeys on the street I'm afraid my goods will be confiscated. You know oil is hard to find nowadays, and it means everything to me. My wife and my seven children are waiting for me at home, with the profits from selling my oil. This oil is our bread." And to illustrate his words, he inserted the measuring device inside one of the vessels on the first donkey and took it out totally full. "I'll fill your oil jar as a means of payment for your hospitality."

With this last argument, Ali Baba was completely sure that lodging the merchant under his roof was very convenient. He made him come inside the yard and showed him where he could leave the donkeys, at the stable. Once the animals were settled in, he invited the merchant to come inside the house.

"Oh, no, no, I don't want to bother you. I'd rather stay here, at the stable, with the donkeys. Don't worry about me, I'm very tired and I'll go to sleep right away."

Ali Baba was puzzled that the man rejected his hospitality, but he didn't insist too much. He thought that maybe the merchant wanted to rest near his dear merchandise and keep an eye on it.

Then, as he didn't want to make a fool of himself,
he told the Americans that things went wrong
at the last moment and they had
to kill the whole family.

When he got into the house, Ali Baba told Morgana, who was cooking, what happened. The woman agreed with her husband about lodging the merchant.

"When I finish cooking I will bring him some broth."

After telling his children not to go to the stable and bother their guest, Ali Baba went out to run an errand.

"Don't take too long. Dinner's almost ready," his wife said as he went out. And she went on with her pots and pans. After straining the broth, she filled a bowl and went to offer it to the merchant. But when she was near the door, she heard some voices. Very slowly, she approached.

"We'll wait until everybody's asleep to make a move," she heard a man's voice whisper.

"But it is very uncomfortable here, inside the vessels, Inspector," complained one of the hidden policemen.

"Sshhh! Shut up! Do you want them to discover us?"

Morgana had heard more than enough to know what was going on. That man was not a merchant; he was someone who intended to take them during the night. May Allah have mercy on them! What could they do? The situation reminded her of the famous tale of the forty thieves hidden inside forty vessels.

"All right then, I'll do the same thing that the main character of the tale did! I'll be shrewd!" she said, once she recovered from the fright.

Very quietly, she returned to the kitchen, and instead of a bowl of broth, she prepared a big platter of food, where she put everything she had cooked for the family dinner. Then, she took a narcotic made out of opium, which she used in tiny doses as a household remedy for insomnia and pain, and mixed it with the food. She went to the stable with this wonderful meal. Before she came in, she shouted to make sure she'd be heard.

"Mister Merchant! I've brought you some dinner. May I come in?"

She heard some quick movements inside the stable. The sly men were returning to their hiding places.

"Yes, one moment... one moment, please. I must put on my clothes."

Of course, it was an excuse. Who would take off their clothes to sleep in a stable that was as cold as a fridge?

"You may come in now," the would-be merchant finally said.

Morgana came in with the platter in her hands. When he saw what she was offering him, Inspector Fahad was impressed with the hospitality.

"That's too much food, woman. There's enough food to feed a whole army."

"My husband told me that you were very tired, and that tomorrow you must go to the marketplace in Kazimiyah, which is twelve miles away from here. You must recover your strength."

"But this is too much."

"At home, we like to treat our guests as though they were princes. Your gratitude honors us. You must leave nothing on the platter, or else we'll feel offended."

"There's nothing I'd like less than to offend you," said the impostor feeling some remorse.

"Eat at will and sleep well. I'll come tomorrow to take away the empty plates."

Morgana left the stable and closed the door, praying she had planned it out well. When Ali Baba arrived, she told him what she had found out and what she had done. If everything went the way she expected, the fake merchant would share the food with his men. Shortly after that they would

The escape was valuably assisted by the four patient donkeys: they carried all the household furnishings on their backs.

all be sound asleep and Ali Baba and his family could escape.

And that is exactly how things went. Indeed, Inspector Fahad shared the copious dinner with his men, just as Morgana had imagined, and they fell asleep so fast that they couldn't hear any of the preparations for their escape, which was valuably assisted by the four patient donkeys: they carried all the household furnishings on their backs. Again, Morgana's wit saved the family from a tricky situation. The next day, when Inspector Fahad and his men woke up, they found that the house was empty and a note that read: "Bon appétit!" When the Inspector realized he had been deceived, he got really angry. But, as he thought about it, he started to calm down and to feel regard for the courage and cleverness of the woman. There even came a point when he found the situation funny. He deserved that punishment, for trying to do wrong to good people. Then, as he didn't want to make a fool of himself, he told the Americans that things went wrong at the last moment and they had to kill the whole family. They did it so quietly that no neighbor had noticed a thing. This way, he hoped, the Americans would forget about Ali Baba and his family.

With that lie, which he shared with his men (as they didn't want to look like fools either!), Inspector Fahad felt his conscience was clean and he felt satisfied. Of course, without the chocolate. "Our deal didn't include killing them all," the Americans told him. "It was a case of *force majeure*," he answered, just as he had heard them say so many times.

Time went by. Ali and Morgana grew old and lived in poverty, but peacefully, in Jordan. When their time came to an end, death would find them in peace with themselves because they had complied with all the precepts of their religion, trying not to harm anyone and helping the needy.

ALADDIN
AND THE MAGIC LAMP

A LADDIN was a boy who had been born in a modest family. He was twelve years old and full of life. His father died during the war and his mother worked for a tailor. They lived in the Rusafa district, in the old part of Baghdad, very close to the Tigris river. The school he went to was old and cold. The walls were bare, except for a large portrait of the President. Some windows had been broken months ago, but nobody replaced the glass. His teacher was a fat, old woman who didn't scold them much in spite of their frequent mischief. The woman always looked tired and neither Aladdin nor his classmates could understand it: they were so eager to run and jump! But, every once in a while, a classmate didn't go to school one day, and he never came back. Then, the games stopped and their looks clouded over, although they did not understand very well what was going on. He asked his mother why suddenly a kid would stop going to school, and he always got the same answer: "He died out of hunger, fear, or sorrow." Aladdin was quiet and sad for a few days, but it didn't last long, and he finally recovered his desire to go out and play.

Sometimes, when school was out, a group of kids went to Mustansiriyah. It had been a very important university during the times of the Abbasids, the old dynasty of caliphs that settled in Baghdad. There, people could learn about the latest discoveries in the fields of astronomy, pharmacy or medicine. The kids sneaked into the inside courtyard and sniffed around through the classroom windows.

On many afternoons, Aladdin and his friends jumped on the rooftop of the madrasah and spent a long time looking at the river from there. The Tigris divided the town in two, and there were ten bridges to cross it from one bank to the other, which were always full of cars, trucks, bicycles and carts. The many wars had destroyed them, and the inhabitants of Baghdad stubbornly rebuilt them over and over again. From their spot, the sunset dyed the roofs of the houses and the minarets of the mosques a deep red. Sometimes, before they

The school he went to was old and cold. The walls were bare, except for a large portrait of the President. Some windows had been broken months ago, but nobody replaced the glass.

knew it, it got dark. They returned home late in the evening and found their mothers with a long face because it was so late.

"I told you I don't want you to be on the streets so late!" shouted Aladdin's mother, and he lowered his head in repentance.

Apart from the hours he spent at school, Aladdin loved to go to the nearby marketplace, where he loved to take handfuls of leftover fruits and vegetables. And he always remained open mouthed watching a blacksmith shape a piece of iron, or a shoemaker repair a shoe, or a scribe write a letter for somebody who didn't know how. He wished to learn a lot at school so he could write all the letters he wanted to. During the evenings, after a frugal dinner with his mother, Aladdin went to the bank of the Tigris and walked around watching the restaurants braise the fish, which were open and pierced with a stick, the way fish had always been cooked in that region. He went along Abu Nuwas Street, from the Jumhuriyah bridge to the July 14th bridge; those were their names in Saddam's times, and they kept on calling them that. He didn't eat anything, but the act of smelling had become an extraordinary pleasure for him; he opened his nostrils wide, inhaled deeply, let the smells penetrate deep into his nose, almost to his stomach… and he felt happy. Then, he walked to the pier, where there was a monument to Scheherazade, the heroin of the tales of *One Thousand and One Nights*.

One evening, as he was watching a fisherman, he noticed there was a shiny object near the water. He approached very carefully, took it, and when he had it in his hand, he saw it was a lamp. It was not too big and seemed to be made of copper. Then, he remembered the tale his mother told him when he was little before he went to sleep. 'Genies don't exist nowadays!' Aladdin said to himself. But he could not resist rubbing the lamp, softly at first, and then more vigorously. 'Even if I don't get anything else, at least I'll make it shinier before I take it home and give it to my mother,' he thought. But he had the fright of his life when, suddenly, the lamp started to get hot and release thick smoke, producing a rumbling noise like boiling water, until, finally, a genius came out of it. It couldn't be true; things like that only happened in fairytales! Aladdin rubbed his eyes, pinched his cheeks to make sure he was awake and stared, astonished, at the genie, who was still sitting in front of him.

"Master," said that strange figure, bowing his head, "I thank you for taking me out of the darkness. It's been hundreds of years since someone took me out of the lamp!"

"Are you really a genie or am I dreaming?" Aladdin asked, still feeling a little bit scared.

"No," the genie answered. "This is no dream. Genies have existed since the world began, and we always will. Our task is to serve our masters."

"To serve me?" Aladdin asked incredulously. "How can you serve me?"

Then, the genie told him that he could grant three wishes, but that he could not ask for really important things because he was not a first class genie.

"What do you mean you are not a first class genie?"

"It is very easy. The same way there are first, second and third class teams in football, the world of genies is exactly the same: there are different class genies. If we can make important contributions to the wellbeing of the world through our masters' wishes, we get promoted."

"And who decides that?"

"The Board of Remarkable Genies."

The more Aladdin heard, the more surprised he was. No, it couldn't be true. But, what if it was? The best way to find out was to make him prove it.

"If I make a wish now, can you grant it?"

*Aladdin rubbed his eyes, pinched his cheeks
to make sure he was awake and stared, astonished,
at the genie, who was still sitting in front of him.*

"As long as it's a small wish..."

"How small?"

"Well... Let me tell you a few things you cannot ask for, so you'll understand. I have no power over the lives and deaths of people, nor can I move you from one place to another, nor make you rich, nor eliminate a murderer, nor prevent a war from happening..."

Aladdin shrugged his shoulders and asked, "What can you do, then?"

The genie said he could grant him many favors that didn't necessarily have to be such extraordinary things. And he told him to think of his everyday life, what he, his mother, his friends did. Then, Aladdin knew at once what his wish was going to be.

"Can I gobble up a fish like the ones those people over there are eating right now?" he asked pointing toward a nearby restaurant.

"Certainly!"

He hadn't finished pronouncing these words when Aladdin found before him a big tray with a recently cooked carp on it. It was open from top to bottom, seasoned with salt and spices and smelled delicious.

"My goodness!" he exclaimed. And he started to eat it without a second to waste.

When he had been eating for a while, taking care not to burn his fingers, he took a deep breath and thought he would keep the rest of the fish for his mother. In fact, he was stuffed. He raised his head and looked at the genie, who wore a smile of satisfaction.

"If I make another wish, will you grant it?"

Then the genie explained to him how the General Rules of Wish Granting worked. He could make three wishes, just as they had always done.

"Haven't you read a fairytale in your life?" the genie scolded him. He could either do it all at once, or little by little. However, the wish granting was not permanent: once the three first wishes were fulfilled, he couldn't ask for another one for three months. He needed to recharge his batteries!

Aladdin was a practical boy and he thought it would be better to think hard about what his next two wishes would be. He told the genie he was finished for now, and the genie got back into the lamp. The boy returned home holding the object tightly with one hand and half the fish with the other. When his mother saw that wonderful piece of cooked carp that was still quite warm, she felt very happy. Her son told her that he had been given the fish in a restaurant, and the woman believed him. He didn't want to tell her that it was the result of having found the lamp because it would be his secret.

That night, Aladdin almost couldn't sleep. The very next day, at school, he told the story to his best friend, Jamil, a boy that had seen one of his sisters die as a result of a bomb when she was coming home from school, and then lost one of his brothers when he went to play football with his friends and never came back. It was his mother who was ill now. The woman had been eating so little so that her two remaining children would have something to eat, that when she caught the flu she became very sick. For this reason, Jamil asked Aladdin:

"Do you think this genie could get me some medicine for my mother?" Aladdin knew it at once: this was a very good reason to make his second wish. So, when school was out, they went to a place far from the river, Aladdin rubbed the lamp and the genie came out again. Then, he asked for antibiotics for Jamil's mother.

"Oh, antibiotics, antibiotics," the genie complained. "You two think this is very easy, don't you? But I cannot make a truck full of antibiotics appear. They are scarce, even for a genie."

"How many could you get for us?" begged Jamil.

"Five boxes, maximum, for each wish."

The two friends looked into each other's eyes, nodded and Aladdin just said a word:

"Done!"

And right then and there, five big boxes of antibiotics appeared on top of a flat rock right before their eyes. Jamil took them quickly, hugged Aladdin and went running to his house.

The third wish was a sewing machine for his mother. He knew that he wouldn't be able to ask for anything else for another three months. His mother, using her sewing machine, could work better and faster. But the best part was that, with the medicines, Jamil's mother was able to recover, although not completely. After three months, Aladdin made his wishes again. Knowing the limitations, he asked for things as normal as a box of fruit, clothes, more medicine for Jamil's mother or for some neighbor who needed them, and cans of gasoline that he sold at some traffic lights.

Days and months passed, but going out in the street was still very dangerous. A bomb could explode on every corner, mosque, market or even in front of a school. Tomorrow was an unknown word in Baghdad; people only lived the moment.

The Americans said they were invading the

country in order to overthrow the dictator, but they stayed and occupied it. There had been elections, but violence had not stopped. Since then, Bin Laden's friends had been having a great time making bombs explode here and there. Instead of getting better, everything was worse than before, since besides the foreign soldiers, there was the Iraqi army, and the squads (nobody knew where they came from) that killed people and made them disappear. Aladdin had seen many of his schoolmates orphaned due to the death or disappearance of their families; then, since they had no way to make a living, they fell into the hands of criminal gangs that exploited and treated them poorly. He had sometimes found a little girl, who was one of his orphan neighbors and was his age, sniffing glue next to a traffic light, and he had felt terribly sorry. Thus, his next wish for the genie was to help that little girl.

Sometimes only two or three of his twenty classmates went to school. One day, as he was leaving school, he saw a car stop, four men got out and took a little girl, Jadija. She was only ten, and her parents had to sell their house and their car in order to pay for the ransom to her kidnappers.

Four times a year, Aladdin made his wishes to the genie. He got used to planning everything very

His mother, using her sewing machine,
could work better and faster.

carefully, and he thought long and hard about what he would ask for. A few years went by like this. Many boys and girls had died in Baghdad, at first due to confiscations, while there was no lack of food at the dictator's palaces, and then due to the invasion and subsequent occupation by the British and American troops. Aladdin thought that it didn't matter who was in charge, whether it was a tyrant with a general's stripes, a monarch with a crown on his head or a civilian approved by the occupying forces, things would go wrong all the same. He had sometimes thought that Allah was on vacation somewhere in the Western World because it was not fair.

Finally, with the help of the genie and his little favors, Aladdin managed to go to the university, which had lost its past splendor. Now, teachers were continuously murdered and the conditions for studying were very precarious. However, Aladdin put a lot of effort into becoming one of the best law students. Jamil had grown older too; his mother and his brothers had been saved thanks to the medicine the genie had been giving them, and he now worked at the office of a military quarter at the airport.

It certainly a pleasant job, but he hadn't done very well at school and he had to accept the first thing he found. "And I can say I'm lucky," he said, resigned, "because there are many unemployed people." He talked a lot with Aladdin about the job before he accepted it. His friend didn't like it either, but he knew it was very hard to make a living, and it was necessary to work somewhere. Some acquaintances accused Jamil of being a traitor, of cooperating with the invading forces, but he replied that if those people owned everything now, it didn't make a difference where you worked. And he had to earn a living, right?

Although it was mostly used by the Iraqi troops, the military quarter was actually run by an American battalion. Sometimes Aladdin went to pick up Jamil at his workplace and they went for a walk together along the banks of the Tigris, the way they did when they were little kids. One day, when he was waiting for his friend outside the entrance, he saw a jeep go out that was driven by an American woman soldier. The car stopped for a moment before pulling into the main road, so Aladdin could see her perfectly: she was a young woman, with a round, tanned face and very big eyes. She noticed she was being watched and turned around to see him too. Then, instead of finding the arrogant, disdainful look that the occupants usually had, Aladdin came face to face with a strong, tender look, a look that touched his heart. He was so impressed that when his friend arrived, he couldn't stop asking him questions: "Who is she? What's her name? What does she do? Where is she from? Does she go outside every day? What time does she come out?"

"You have too many questions, and I have no answer for them," said Jamil, who didn't know the girl at all.

From that day on, Aladdin couldn't get that girl out of his mind. One day, at the university, he confessed his love to a classmate, who was scandalized.

"Have you fallen in love with an American woman? How could you do something like that? Those people have no hearts; they are murderers. Have you forgotten about what they did to our parents and to us?"

That boy was a member of the resistance, and Aladdin thought he might be right, but he couldn't stop thinking about the American girl. He was madly in love. 'There must be some good Americans,' he said to himself.

Jamil became his "cupid," and supplied him with information. He already knew that the girl's name was Susan, she was an orphan, and she had been born in Mexico. She was what they called a *latino* girl, and she was not married.

"What else? Tell me more about her," Aladdin said, always wanting more information. "Could you give her a note I have written?"

And that's what Jamil did. As an introduction, he limited himself to sending her an English translation of some verses taken from the poem *The Rain Song*, by the poet Al Jayyab.

While he was waiting for an answer, the world stopped, and the hours were eternal. He hardly eat, and his performance at university declined. He was so in love! But days went by and no answer came from his beloved. So he anxiously made the genie come out of the lamp and asked him to intervene.

"Who do you think I am? A matchmaker? I do not have people wed!" the genie said, irate with his demand.

"But there must be something you can do to make her pay attention to me."

"I will only give you a piece of good advice: keep on writing poems. Women love poetry, even if they are soldiers."

Aladdin followed the genie's advice, and when eight days had passed since he had started to write a poem a day to his loved one without getting an answer, Jamil came out of work with a huge smile in his face.

"She asked me today who you are, how you know her, how long have been friends, and where you work."

"And what did you tell her?"

"I praised you to the heavens."

Aladdin was in ecstasy. Jamil had talked to Susan about him and he said that the girl had listened to him very attentively.

"Then, I asked her if she wanted to write something for you, and she said that she was going to think about it, and that maybe she would."

In rapture, Aladdin kissed his friend and started to jump and dance around.

"You are totally crazy. She only said she was going to think about it..."

"That's enough for me. If she thinks about me, I'm happy."

Susan didn't think about it for too long, and the very next day, Jamil took the answer to his friend. It was a letter where she just repeated the questions she had asked Jamil the day before. Immediately after he got home, Aladdin began to write a long answer, telling her about his family, his studies, his hopes...

From that moment on, the letters between Aladdin and Susan grew in frequency, until one day they arranged to meet in a coffeehouse in Baghdad. Aladdin had chosen a neutral place, a place that would neither be full of foreigners nor only full of Iraqi people, so they wouldn't feel uncomfortable. Aladdin was so nervous that half an hour before their meeting, he was already seated at a table, before a glass of tea and smoking a hookah. When Susan finally showed up, to him it seemed as though the sky had burst into a symphony of wonderful colors. All the voices hushed, all the movements stopped. It was only him and her. The woman was wearing a handkerchief around her head in order to go unnoticed and not to attract attention. She sat down in front of Aladdin and, for the very first time, he could look at her from a close-up: she had dark skin, her face was round and her eyes could almost speak.

At first they both felt a little timid. They actually knew a lot about each other because of their letters, but it was so different to be facing one another. She told him that she had had doubts until the last moment. She had not talked about this to anyone at the quarter because she was afraid they wouldn't understand and it could cause her trouble. She didn't even know if she understood it either. He told her too that he was afraid some of his friends would never approve of him talking to an American girl. He suggested they go for a walk along the bank of the Tigris, and that's what they did.

Walking there, Aladdin felt safer. Nobody could hear them, they could see the sky, the now forsaken and dirty banks; but that was his territory. Then he started to tell her about the pranks he played with his friends by the river when he was a little kid.

"One day, Jamil and I put some curcuma root into the tea a friend of ours was drinking because he had played a dirty trick on us and tradition has it that, if you drink curcuma root, your moustache won't ever grow again. And, as you may have already seen, Iraqis love to grow their moustaches."

She listened attentively and smiled, but she lacked the joy Aladdin would have liked to see.

"Can you imagine, his face turning all white and pale?" Aladdin laughed, showing his white teeth, as he tried to make her smile.

Then she told him that she felt very lonely; she had been there for ten months and she was the only woman in the battalion. Her mates had often bothered her, and on one occasion, one of them even tried to sexually assault her. She was looking forward to going back to her country and to doing something else.

"Why did you become a soldier, then?"

"*Time has flown at your side.
Will we see each other again?*"

"Because I was unemployed and I needed a job. Becoming a professional soldier is a way to make a living. You'll see very few rich men in the army. The people who join the army are the ones who don't have many job opportunities. We think this is a good solution, but we are wrong. You must be a certain type of person in order to like this, and I'm not that type of person."

"And what did you know about my country?" Aladdin asked.

"I knew it was governed by a very cruel dictator who had teamed up with Bin Laden in order to expand terrorism all over the world."

"That's not true!" he complained.

Then, Aladdin told her that Saddam Hussein was certainly a cruel dictator, but he had never teamed up with Bin Laden because they belonged to very different ethnic groups and Islamic movements. Bin Laden came from Saudi Arabia, a country allied to the Americans that turned against them for obscure reasons. It wasn't true either that Saddam Hussein had weapons of mass destruction at the time that the war began. He had owned them in the past, that is true, but most of them he had bought from the Americans when they were allies.

"This war has actually had only one reason: the

control over Iraqi petroleum," Aladdin finally said. "Peace? They couldn't care less about peace. Take a look at how we are now, if you don't believe me. There are dozens of deaths every day, and terrorism has increased. It is now that Bin Laden is doing as he pleases, in Iraq and all over the world."

Susan didn't know anything about all that. She was locked up at the quarter and went out to make the rounds when she was supposed to. She had sometimes seen and heard things that didn't quite match with what their superiors had told them: that they were there to save Iraq, that the whole world was on their side, that the Iraqi people were waiting for them and that they would be received with open arms. But some things happened that made her doubt. And her doubts ate at her conscience and left her mortified.

It was late, and Susan had to return to the quarter. Aladdin looked at her tenderly and said, "Time has flown at your side. Will we see each other again?"

And they saw each other again. Through their personal postman, as Susan called Jamil, they went on exchanging letters. Their walks along the banks of the Tigris became a customary thing. However, they very often felt powerless because of the people who had died during terrorist attacks. Susan was very scared. Aladdin remained silent, and looking up, he held her hand tightly and walked by her side in silence. Too often they could see a smoke column in the sky from a fire provoked by a bomb. The more they got to know each other, the more they respected each other; respect brought familiarity, and familiarity brought love. Susan eventually fell in love with that shy, plain, intelligent boy that was showing her the other face of his country and his people's reality. And, with this discovery, her fear and rejection towards her military mates grew greater and greater. She didn't even talk to them outside of work.

One day news came that Susan's battalion was being relieved. When he heard about it, Aladdin told her to stay. Her body shivered when she thought of the desolating city of Baghdad, but she loved Aladdin and, after giving it much thought, she accepted to stay. Nobody was waiting for her in her country. In fact, she had always felt treated as a foreigner. 'If I have to be a foreigner in both countries, at least here I have a man who loves me,' she thought. And she didn't return to the United States.

Aladdin's mother took Susan in and loved her as her own child. From that moment on, what Aladdin always asked the genie once every three months was: 'Help us as much as you can!'

Maybe someday there would only be the moon and stars shining in that sky. No more planes. No more bombs.

He didn't want to take advantage of him. The genie, who was happy with a master who demanded so little and who was content with a couple of books, a few meters of cloth or a dozen spools of thread, always pleased him.

He firmly believed that he was going to be promoted by grace of that wise and good hearted boy. Whether it was thanks to the genie or maybe simply as a result of his perseverance, Aladdin finished his studies with very good qualifications. Susan learned how to sew with her mother-in-law's sewing machine and became an excellent tailor. The country continued suffering great hardship. It was hard to go on after so much devastation, but they had each other and that was what mattered.

Aladdin understood a little better what they called America, and Susan also understood better and better what in the past had been known as Mesopotamia. They had two sons and a daughter, and at night, they all climbed together to their house's rooftop and watched the sky. Maybe someday there would only be the moon and stars shining in that sky. No more planes. No more bombs. No more blood.

Maybe the genie would have already been promoted by then, and with a first class genie, Aladdin could do wonders.

THE END

جلوريا أريمون

حكايات من بغداد

مجموعة "Ursa Maior"

حكايات من بغداد
العدد الأول 2010
العنوان الأصلي: Contes de Bagdad

حقوق الطبع 2010، جلوريا أريمون فينتورا
حقوق الطبع 2010، علي بابا، جلوريا أريمون فينتورا ويوسف لورمان رويج
حقوق الطبع لهذا العدد: ICG Marge, SL
ترجمة إلى الإنجليزية: إفا كانيادا
ترجمة إلى العربية: فادي هديب
الرسوم التوضيحية للغلاف: هيلانة رويز
صورة الغلاف: جلوريا أريمون فينتورا

الناشر: Marge Books – شارع فالينثيا 558، الطابق العلوي 2 – 08026 برشالونا، اسبانيا
هاتف: 130 449 34-932+ فاكس: 865 310 34-932+ الموقع الألكتروني: www.marge.es

مدير النشر: ديفيد سولير
المحررين: هيكتور سولير، لورا ماتوس، آنا بالاثيوس
تحرير: ساندرا مارتينيز
شارك في التحرير: ليانه فيرلي
محرر الإنتاج: ميغيل آنجل رويج
محرر الهامش: مرسيدس لارا
طبع من قبل: Més Gran Serveis Gràfics i Digitals (سانتا كولوما دي ثيرفيلو)

جلوريا أريمون

بالتعاون مع يوسف لورمان

حكايات من بغداد

هذه العدد هو جزء من مشروع التعليم من أجل السلام:

بدعم من:

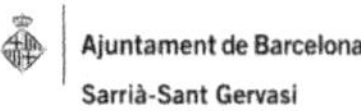

MARGE BOOKS

ملتزمون مع العالم (*Compromesos amb el món*) هي عبارة عن منظمة غير حكومية صغيرة، تأسست في عام 2007 في كاتالونيا. نقوم بدعم وتعزيز مشاريع التعاون الدولي. التعليم الهادف إلى السلام هو واحد من أهدافنا الرئيسية. نقدم هذا الكتاب إلى جميع المنظمات التي تعمل من أجل ذات الهدف.

للمعلومات والاتصال: www.compromesos.cat.

ملاحظة:

إذهب، إلى www.marge.es لجمع بعض المقترحات الموجهة للذين يرغبون في العمل على المشاكل التي يعيشها العراق، ولمناقشة العادات والتقاليد والقيم والتي تهدف إلى التعليم من أجل السلام.

الفهـــــرس

قيدوا بالسلاسل أمواج دجلة .
كيف سنحلم اليوم بالسفر؟
و إلى أية جزيرة سنذهب؟

سركون بولص "شاعر عراقي"

الحكايات التي سنعرضها في هذا الكتاب، تتركز على ثلاث شخصيات من حكايات ألف ليلة وليلة، وحكايات ألف ليلة وليلة لها أصول مختلفة.

فأقدم القصص أتت من الهند، والقصص من الأصل الفارسي تشكل مجموعة أخرى، وهناك مجموعة ثالثة، تشمل الحكايات ذو الطابع الاسلامي والتي أتت من العراق، وأخيراً، هناك مجموعة رابعة من الحكايات الموجودة في مصر.

هناك وثائق عديدة مكتوبة باللغة العربية منذ القرن التاسع. وفي العام 1704 نشر فرانسيس غالاند، أول مجلد مترجم، وهكذا وصلت هذه الوثائق إلى الشعوب ألاوروبية بنجاح

كبير. ولذلك قاموا بإدراج قصص جديدة في القرن التاسع عشر، مثل السندباد البحار، وفي وقت لاحق قاموا بإدراج بعض القصص الأخرى، والتي إنتشرت بشكل منفصل، مثل علي بابا والأربعين حرامي ومصباح علاء الدين السحري.

وتبدأ حكاية ألف ليلة وليلة عندما يكتشف حاكم بغداد؛ الملك شهريار، أن زوجته تقوم بخداعه مع رجل آخر. ومن شدة غضبه، يقرر، أن يجلب الى سريره كل يوم فتاة نبيلة عذراء، ويقوم بقتلها مع شروق الشمس. وتلعب شهرزاد إبنة أحد الوزاراء، الشخصية الرئيسية للحكايات، وذلك عندما تعتزم إنهاء القتل اليومي للفتيات. ولذلك، تطلب لقاء الملك لتقص عليه في كل ليلة حكاية، ولا تنهيها حتى شروق الشمس، وبهذه الطريقة لن يقتلها الملك لأنه يريد معرفة نهاية القصة، ولذلك فعليه إنتظار حلول الليل لإكمال الإستماع. وتحوي الحكايات مواضيع شيقة ومختلفة، مثل: الحب، الروائع، المغامرات، المؤامرات وشجاعة الفرسان.

أما قصص السندباد وعلي بابا وعلاء الدين، فكانت عبارة عن إضافة للقصص القديمة، ونحن موجودون في العراق اليوم، لأن أرض هذا البلد تتزامن بجزء من الذي كان معروفاً في العصور القديمة بإسم بلاد ما بين النهرين؛ نهري دجلة

والفرات، اللذان يصبان في الخليج الفارسي. ومنذ أكثر من 5500 عام، تم إختراع أحد أولى أشكال الكتابة في تلك البلاد.

وفي عام 1990 عندما هاجمت أمريكا وبريطانيا العراق، قامت بقصف المرافق الهامة وعلى رأسها مصانع الورق العراقية، وفرضت الأمم المتحدة حظر على التسويق الخارجي، وكانت الفنون التخطيطية والرسم والطباعة من بعض المنتجات العراقية المحظورة. وفي الوقت ذاته، حظرت إستخدام أقلام الرصاص للكتابة، مع الحجة القائلة بأنها تحتوي على مادة الجرافيت، التي يمكن أن تكون قابلة للاستخدام العسكري.

وعلى مر التاريخ، وفي جميع أنحاء العالم عاش الفتيان والفتيات بتجارب الحب والمغامرة، وذلك في أماكن مختلفة جداً عن الأماكن التي نعيش فيها نحن. فكلنا نتشارك الرغبة في التعلم واللعب والمرح والحب.... فمنذ عدة سنوات يعيش الشباب العراقي حياة مختلفة عن التي نعيشها نحن، وذلك بسبب الحروب، وبسبب ذلك الدكتاتور أولاً، وثانياً بسبب الاحتلال الأمريكي للعراق.

خلال السنوات الأولى للإحتلال، قُتل مئات الآلاف من الناس،

وكان الثلث من القاصرين، وتتشرد العديد منهم وهاجر إلى خارج البلاد واحد من بين كل ثمانية أشخاص.

العاصمة بغداد، ليست متصلة بالبحر، ولذلك فإن المخرج الوحيد للخليج الفارسي يكون عن طريق البصرة؛ المدينة المتواجدة في الجنوب وبعد أن يكون قد إلتقى نهري دجلة والفرات معاً. وفي هذه المدينة وما قبل الإحتلال، كان هنالك تمثال في الشارع يمثل السندباد وهو يراقب البحر.

في بغداد، وفي ساحة كبيرة، هنالك عدد من التماثيل التي تمثل علي بابا والأربعين حرامي، وبعض الشخصيات الأسطورية الموجود في جميع أنحاء البلاد.

العام 2002 في البصرة، تعارفت على فتيين يعملان في تنظيف الأحذية، كانا يعملان في الصباح ويذهبان إلى المدرسة في المساء. وقالوا لي بأنهم سعداء. ومن على مسافة بعيدة، وبعد مرور زمن طويل، أتذكرهم في كثير من الأحيان، فضلاً عن المناظر الطبيعية للعراق، كالصحراء، الأراضي الخصبة، السواحل واطلال الحضارات القديمة... وخصوصاً نظرات الفتيان والفتيات في الطرقات.

كلنا نريد أن نعيش بسعادة مثل الشخصيات التي في القصص منذ عدة قرون. فأنا لا أستطيع ولا أريد أن أنسى ذالك اليوم،

عندما أغمضت عيني وبدأت في تخيل الابطال القدامى؛ السندباد، علي بابا وعلاء الدين... والملابس ومشاكل الشباب في العراق اليوم.

ومن هنا نشأت هذه القصص التي فيها تعيش نظرات منظفي الأحذية، ونظرات الأطفال وهم يلعبون في ساحات المساجد، والذين يدرسون في المدرسة أو الذين يرقدون في أسرّة المستشفيات.

وتمثل قصص ألف ليلة وليلة إنتصار الفن والثقافة على الهمجية، والتي أدت في نهاية المطاف وبعد ليال طوال من الإستماع للقصص، إلى أن يغفر الملك عن حياة شهرزاد، من خلال الكلمة، الكلمة التي تحولت الى حقيقة. ومن هنا، نتمنى أن تساعدنا **حكايات من بغداد** على فهم أن الكلمة والحق، هي الأسلحة الوحيدة التي يجب أن نستخدمها في الصراعات والنزاعات.

ما يحدث الآن في العراق ونشاهده تقريبا بشكل مباشر من خلال التلفاز، يجعلنا نخاطر على أن نعتاد على رؤية آلام الآخرين، وأن نكون في مأمن من المعاناة والموت.

نأمل أن تكون قراءة هذه القصص، مع التأمل والخيال، أن تساعدنا في استعادة الواقع.

وإلى جميع الشباب، يمكننا أن نغير الواقع، فكل شيء يعتمد علينا.

جلوريا أريمون

سندباد

المكان جميل جداً، حيث يوجد فيه نهري دجلة والفرات، وكما يقال أنها كانت الجنة على الأرض. تجري الماء في كل مكان تشكل الأنهار والجداول والقنوات والبحيرات. وهناك كانت أشجار الفاكهة بجميع أنواعها: المشمش والبرتقال والتفاح والكمثرى... وخاصة أشجار النخيل طويلة الجذوع، وقطوف التمر الحلوة معلقة على تاجها. ولم يفتقد هذا المكان الجميل من الحيوانات، فكان هناك: الطيور والخيول والحمير والماعز والأغنام والقطط والخفافيش... وفي هذه المنطقة حيث يلتقي النهرين كانت هناك بلدة صغيرة، تسمى القرنة، ومن هناك تشكل نهر شط العرب، وطوله مائة كيلومتر تقريباً بإتجاه الجنوب، ويصب في الخليج الفارسي. وهذا النهر عميق، بحيث يسمح بمرور السفن الكبيرة الآتية من البحر.

في العام 637، وبين قنوات المياه وبساتين النخيل، بنى أحد الخلفاء مدينة؛ البصرة: التي تقع في أسفل النهر، والتي سرعان ما سكنها الآلاف من الناس، وبالقرب من البحر قام ببناء ميناء: أم قصر، لترسوا فيها قوارب صيد السمك وسفن التنقل. وفي غضون سنوات قليلة، وصل هؤلاء الرجال إلى الصين، وأبحروا إلى ما وراء الحدود، إكتشفوا آفاق جديدة، وعوالم مختلفة الألوان والأذواق، نظرات ولغات وحب...

وبعد عدة قرون، سكن في البصرة شاب طويل القامة، داكن البشرة، إسمه سندباد، عيونه كبيرة ومستديرة وشعره أسود وأجعد. حامد، أحد أعمامه، بشرته جافة ومتجعدة لمرور السنين، وبدأت التجاعيد بالظهور عندما توفيت أمه أثناء الولادة في الابن الثاني. توفي والده قبل بضعة أشهر فقط، فقد أصيب بحمى شديدة، وفي غضون أسابيع قليلة غير المرض ذلك الرجل القوي المعافي إلى رجل هزيل من اللحم والجلد.

وكان يقضي سندباد يومه في الشارع، أولاً يلعب مع الأطفال، وبعد اللعب كان يذهب ويبحث عن لقمة العيش. وغالباً ما كان يذهب إلى النهر لإلقاء نظرة على الجزر الصغيرة وسط صخب المياه والسفن التجارية المارة. وكل مرة وعلى نحو متزايد، كانت تصل السفن من الخارج،

في السنوات الأولى أبحر سندباد على متن سفينة، والتي كان يعمل عليها كمساعد.

بعضها ممتلئة ببضائع لم تكن موجودة عندهم، وأخرى على متنها رجال من مختلف الأجناس والألوان. ففي أحد الأيام وعندما أكمل سندباد الثالثة عشرة من عمره وعندما كان يشاهد الرجال الذين ينزلون من السفن، قرّر: "سأكون بحاراً". وهكذا كان. وعمه كان قد مات، وليس لديه أية مسؤولية للاعتناء بأحد. ففي السنوات الأولى عمل سندباد كمساعد على متن سفينة كبيرة، ولكن سرعان ما جمع ما يكفي من المال لشراء سفينة صغيرة يملكها، وهكذا لن يضطر للعمل عند أي مسؤول آخر. وفي وسط البحر، كان يشاهد تحليق طيور النورس؛ فإذا أتى فصل الشتاء كان يحرص على أن تلامس الشمس وجهه وذراعيه؛ وإذا أتى فصل الصيف؛ كان يحرص على أن يحمي جسده تحت مظلة من شدة الحر. وفي وسط البحر، كان سعيداً. أحياناً كان يشعر بوحده وأحياناً بأن لديه رفقه. فيضع الطُعم في الصنارة آملاً أن يصطاد سمكة، فلم يكن في عجلة من أمره كما لو أن الوقت قد توقف. كان سندباد شاب نشيط، يصحوا باكراً في كل يوم، وكان يبدو عليه أنه من السهل جداً الذهاب لصيد السمك كل يوم. فلم يتوقف يوماً عن النظر الى الأفق، وفي المساء، وعندما كان يصل الى كوخه، كان يعد النقود التي جمعها من بيع السمك.

وفي كل ليلة كان يفكر في عدد السنين التي سيعمل بها من أجل جمع مبلغ كبير من المال، ليمكنه من شراء سفينة جيدة، والتي من شأنها أن تسمح له على المضي قدماً. ومعظم الفتيان في عمره؛ الذين يعيشون مع أسرهم، كانوا ينتظرون أن يختار لهم والديهم الفتاة التي سيتزوجوا بها، لكن سندباد لم يكن مستعجلاً. فكان من الواضح أنه معجب بالفتيات، ولكن... أراد أن يؤجل الأمر لوقت لاحق، لأنه كان مقتنع تماماً، أن لديه أمور أهم للقيام بها في الوقت الحالي.

وفي ليلة هادئة، خرج سندباد إلى الشارع، وعكست قناة الماء التي تمر من أمام بيته ضوء القمر المستدير، وعنما كان ينظر إليه كان يعتقد أن القمر يغامزه. أحب سندباد كل شيء من حوله، فكان يشعر هكذا من أعماق قلبه، وكان يتذكر تلك الرحلة والأصدقاء والنهر و سوق السمك وشارع الوزان المزدحم ومآذن المساجد الكثيرة والجسور التي تمر عبر القنوات والمخابز العديدة... ولكن، هناك شيء بحاجة للتغيير!. فمع كل هذه الذكريات ذهب سندباد إلى المقهى ليشرب الشاي مع الأرجيلة وليلتقي مع الأصدقاء. وكما هو الحال دائماً، في المقهى كانوا جميعاً من الرجال، لأن النساء عادةً لا تذهب إلى هناك. وكان هناك رجل مسن يريد أن يبيع

سفينته الشراعية، لأنه لم يعد يستطيع العمل عليها في هذا السن. وكان سندباد يعلم أن سفينة هذا الرجل كانت جيدة وكبيرة، فقدم سندباد عرضاً على الرجل لشراء السفينة، على أن يدفع له مبلغ من المال للبدء في العمل على السفينة وأن يسدد باقي المبلغ خلال السنوات القليلة المقبلة. بعد مناقشة وجدل لفترة من الزمن، تمت المصافحة على الصفقة، كما يفعل الرجال الصالحين. لأن الكلمة كانت تكفي في ذلك الوقت، ولم يلزم توقيع عقود البيع والشراء.

وبعد بضعة أيام، جهز سندباد جِرار الماء وحقائب الطعام، وجهز السفينة للإبحار، لتكون تلك أول مغامرة يقوم بها، وما أن بدأ بالإبحار وبدأت نسمات الريح تهب، كان يراقب المدينة التي بدت أصغر شيئاً فشيئاً كلما إبتعد عنها. وبعد عبور دلتا كبيرة وفي النقطة حيث يلتقي النهر بالبحر، تجاوز الجزر التي كان ينظر إليها دائماً والتي يعرفها عن ظهر قلب، إتجه سندباد شرقاً وترك السفينة تقوده الى حيث ما تشاء. وبما أن الرياح لم تكن قوية، فأبحرت السفينة ببطء لشق طريقها...؛ إلى أن صار البحر هادءً تماماً، والرياح لا تهب إلى أن توقفت السفينة تماماً. سندباد لم يكن خائفاً، واستغل تلك اللحظات من الهدوء لينام أو ليأكل شيئا. ولكن المشكلة كانت عندما هبت الريح في

الإتجاه المعاكس، بحيث أبحرت السفينة في إتجاه لا يريد الذهاب إليه. وبعد ثلاثة أيام من الإبحار وجد نفسه مرة أخرى عند مصب النهر. ثم أدرك أنه لم يكن مستعدا بما فيه الكفاية، وأنه بحاجة لإكتساب المعرفة من الأشخاص الذين أبحروا لسنين عديدة. فذهب وسأل، وتعلم كثيراً من البحارة ذوي الخبرة، وعلى الرغم من أنه لا يستطيع القراءة أو الكتابة، قام برسم بعض الخرائط البدائية. وجمع كل اللوازم، وأخذ صندوق من المجوهرات التي ورثها من العائلة مع بعض المنتجات للبيع. مع هذا الحِمل، أبحر مرة أخرى. ولكن هذه المرة، إتبع توصيات البحارة ذوي الخبرة، وأن لا يبتعد كثيراً عن اليابسة، فذهب في إتجاه السواحل الفارسية. وكانت الرحلة على ما يرام، وكانت الرياح مواتية، وبعد بضعة أيام وصل الى مدينة غير معروفة حيث وجد فيها أناساً يتحدثون لغة أخرى. وعثر على رجل في الميناء، وأخبره هذا الرجل انه في هذه الأماكن تتحدث الناس بطرق تختلف كثيراً، حتى أنه لا يفهم كل منهما الآخر. ومع ذلك، كان الناس الذين إعتادوا على التنقل والإبحار في مختلف البلدان، يستخدمون ذكائهم لفهم غيرهم وجعل أنفسهم مفهومين.

— والأهم من كل ذلك، قال له الرجل، هو أن يكون لديك

الرغبة في التواصل.

خلال الأيام التي قضاها هناك، باع سندباد حمولته من التمر والملح، وإشترى أحد التجار كنز سندباد العائلي الصغير، المكون من عقداً وسواراً وخاتمين. وإشترى سندباد بذلك الحرير وبعض المنتجات الغير متوفرة في بلده من الأموال التي حصل عليها. وبعد أن عاد إلى البصرة، حيث كان قد باع كل شيء وحصل على كيس من المال، قام بتسديد جزء من ديونه، وجزء آخر لشراء المزيد من البضائع للتجارة.

خلال عام واحد، أبحر السندباد مرات عديدة، ذهاباً وإياباً قدر المستطاع عن طريق الموانئ الفارسية للبيع والشراء. وفي كل مرة، كان يبحر أبعد شيئاً فشيئاً وعرف السواحل الفارسية عن ظهر قلب، بداية من المناطق الخضراء الرائعة ومن ثم الصحراء. وفي الماضي، سمع من بعض الأصدقاء، أنه بعد عبور مضيق هرمز، يوجد بحر كبير جداً ويمكن أن يؤدي إلى الهند والصين. وأنهم أبحروا أيضاً من خلال الساحل الغربي لشبه الجزيرة العربية، ولكنهم لم يبحروا أبداً إلى شبه جزيرة قطر، لأن هناك تيارات قوية وخطيرة جداً، وذات مرة، هاجمت القراصنة كل السفن التي أبحرت إلى هذا الساحل، ولذلك يسمونه بساحل القراصنة.

خلال عام واحد، أبحر السندباد مرات عديدة، ذهاباً وإياباً قدر
المستطاع عن طريق الموانئ الفارسية للبيع والشراء

وبعد وقت ليس بطويل، سدد سندباد الدين للرجل المسن الذي كان قد باعه سفينة الشراعية، وقرر أن يتخذ مساعدا له، وكان إسمه بدر الدين.

مع التنقل والسفر، تعلم سندباد كل ما لم يكن يعرفه من قبل، فقد تعرف على كثير من الناس، بعضهم من الذين يُعجبون، والبعض الآخر من الذين يخشون؛ وأنه سيواجه الكثير من المخاطر: العواصف واللصوص والمحتالين؛ الذين يبيعون طائر العقعق بدلاً من طائر الحجل...؛ لكنه كان شابٌ ذكي، فعلى الرغم من انه أميي، لا يقرأ ولا يكتب، إلا أنه إستطاع أن يفهم نصف اللغات التي كان يتحدث بها الناس، حيثما كان؛ فكان مستمعاً جيداً ومتكلماً بارع، وكان يعرف متى يجب عليه أن يصمت، وكان أميناً على حفظ وكتم الأسرار. ففي كل ميناء، كان لديه صديق، وفي كل قرية، كان لديه معجبة تراقبه بهدوء. وفي كل مرة كان يعود فيها إلى البصرة؛ المكان الذي كان يعلم انه الوطن، ولو لوقت قصير. كان يشعر بهزة في الساقين وعدم إتزان في جميع أنحاء جسده. وعندما كان يرى أطراف مآذن المساجد، التي كان يعرفها جيداً، دائماً كان يصرخ:

— أنا بمأمن، فأنا في الوطن!

فسندباد، لا يزال يتذكر بعض القصص التي قصّها عليه عمه، عند الحديث عن جنكيز خان؛ إمبراطور منغوليا، فعندما وصل إلى تلك البلاد لم يترك وراءه سوى الدمار والرعب، وهذه الشعوب مختلفة تماماً عن غيرها من الشعوب، كالعباسيين والآشوريين واليونانيين، الذين جلبوا معهم الثقافة والثروة. وأخبروه، أن الذي كان بلده، أصبح مُحتلاً من قبل الإمبراطورية العثمانية، وفي وقت لاحق إتحدت القبائل لمواجهة العدو المشترك، ألا وهم البريطانيين، الذين كانوا قد إحتلوا هذا المكان وأرادوا أن يملكوه. ولم يكن من السهل عليهم المغادرة. فالجميع قاومهم بطرق شتى...

أثناء الإبحار، كان للسندباد الكثير من الوقت للتفكير، وكان دائماً يتساءل: لماذا لا يمكن للإنسان ان يعيش في سلام، يصيد الأسماك ويعمل بالزراعة والتجارة... ويعيش الحب!؟.

كما قالها سندباد ذات مرّة في أحد المقاهي، فضحك عليه كبار السن، وقالوا له: ستعرف عندما تكبر، فإن كل شخص يفعل ما يحلو له وخاصة الحكام. فهناك عدد قليل من الذين لديهم الكثير من المال، والبقية لا يملكون شيئاً وبالكاد يستطيعون أن يتدبر أمورهم.

ومن ثم، جلس سندباد صامتاً، وكان متفائلاً على أمل العثور

في يوم من الأيام على كنزٍ مخفي في إحدى جزر الخليج. وفي ما مضى أخبر سندباد بذلك شخص يثق به، فأجابه قائلاً: أن أعظم كنز لدينا هنا، النفط. ولكنه لا يخصنا نحن.

حفروا في أعماق الأرض، إلى أعماق أعماق الأرض، وهناك وجدوا الذهب الأسود. وكان السندباد يستخدم النفط لإشعال النار والطهي والتنقل... لكنهم أخبروه كيف هو العالم وكيف يسير ويتطور، وأنه يمكن إستخدام النفط لأشياء كثيرة، ولكن ليس في بلده، لأنها بلاد متأخرة، وإنما في أميركا والجانب الآخر من المحيطات الشاسعة التي تستخدمه في صنع كل شيء؛ "من الإبرة إلى الصاروخ".

محيط..! فكر سندباد، المحيط هو البحر الذي لا ينتهي أبداً، حيث يستغرق أسابيع وأسابيع لتصل فيه إلى اليابسة، وهو المكان الذي تطلق فيه العنان، وفيه بعض العواصف الكبيرة. وبسفينة مثل التي أملك، لن تتحمل أكثر من يومين في ذلك المحيط. أمريكا...، هل من الممكن أن أذهب إلى هناك يوماً ما؟ حلم أبدي. هناك، كان الناس أثرياء ولديهم السفن والسيارات، ويعيشون في منازل جميلة ونظيفة ويرتدون ملابس جيدة، وجميع الأطفال يذهبون إلى المدرسة... وعندما أتم سندباد الثامنة عشرة من عمره، في ذلك الوقت كان

الأطفال في بلده يذهبون إلى المدرسة وكان بإمكانهم الذهاب إلى الطبيب إذا مرضوا...، لأن الحكام لم يكونوا موجودين بعد! بغداد، ومنذ وقت قريب، كانت الرحلة تستغرق ثلاثين ساعة عن طريق البر.

يوم سيئ، حيث سمع سندباد في أحد المقاهي بالسوق، بأن بلاده كانت في حالة حرب مع دولة مجاورة؛ الفرس، والتي كانت تعرف بإسم ايران. فالخلافات قائمة منذ زمن بعيد، لأنهم كانوا دائماً يتقاتلون من أجل حيازة النهر ومنطقة خوزستان، حيث كان هناك نفط.

ـ لماذا؟ سأل سندباد أولئك الرجال الذين كانوا يشربون الشاي ويدخنون الأرجيلة. فنظر إليه الجميع ولكنهم لم يجيبوا. سوى شخص، أجابه: يا بني، إن القرويين لا يعرفون لماذا هم حُكّامنا في حروب... وفي نهاية المطاف، إذا حصل وإن إنتصرنا أو خسرنا، فإننا دائماً سنكون نحن المتضررين.

وهكذا كان. ولم يعد يجرؤ سندباد على الإبحار إلى السواحل الفارسية؛ فأبحر إلى السواحل الغربية، ولكنها أيضاً لم تكن هادئة. وهناك غالباً ما سمع ورأى طيوراً كبيرة تحلق في السماء تقذف لهباً ودخاناً من أفواهها. كانت سنوات صعبة جداً، لأن القنابل وصلت إلى البصرة. ثماني سنوات من

الجحيم، من خلالها لم يبقى أي أسرة على حالها في المدينة، وتم استدعاء الآباء والأمهات والأبناء في سن الخدمة العسكرية لمحاربة البلاد المجاورة، وقصفوا وذبحوا الأمهات والأطفال الصغار في منازلهم، وبدى أن الأسماك قد إختبأت، لأنه كان من الصعب الذهاب للصيد! انتهت تلك الحرب بتساوي، لا من غالب ولا مغلوب، وحصدت مليون من الأموات من كلا الجانبين. وأطراف السفن الغارقة في الميناء كانت شاهداً على الدمار. وبعد ذلك وتكريماً لقتلى الحرب، أمر الحاكم ببناء مئتان وخمسين من التماثيل على شواطئ البصرة، بحيث يمثل كل واحد منها جنرالاً من الذين لقوا حتفهم في المعارك ضد ايران، والذراع الأيمن للتماثيل يشير إلى الجانب الآخر من الشاطئ، وبنظرات جدية والبنادق معلقة على الأكتاف متحدياً العدو.

ولكن قدرة الإنسان على التفاعل والبقاء على قيد الحياة هائلة، فأعاد سكان البصرة بناء المدينة، وأعيد تشيد المساجد وفتح المتاجر مرة أخرى، وأعيد بناء الجسور عبر القنوات، وعادت الحياة إلى الأسواق المليئة بالألوان، وعاد الصيادين والتجار إلى البحر من جديد.

طلب سندباد من زينب أن ترافقه في رحلة بحرية لبضعة أيام،
لكي يشاركها كنزه العظيم؛ ألا وهو البحر.

وأبحر سندباد من جديد، معتمداً على بدر الدين، الصبي الذي كان يساعده، وباع البضاعة في الخارج وإشترى غيرها ليعود ويبيعها في البصرة.

وكان الوقت يمرّ، وما زال سندباد أعزب،

وفي أحد الأيام قال له زملائه بمودة، يجب عليك الحذر، أن يتجاوزك القطار وتبقى أعزب!

ولذلك نصحوا له بأن لا ينتظر أكثر وأن يتزوج، وأخيراً فعل ذلك، وتزوج بفتاة يتيمة مثله، والتي كانت تعيش مع عمتها وابن عمتها. وكان إسمها زينب، وتبلغ من العمر ستة عشر عاماً، وأدت الحرب إلى مقتل والدها وشقيقيها. وكما هو متعارف، طلب سندباد الزواج يد زينب من كبير أسرتها، وفي هذا الحال، كان ابن عمة الفتاة من يقرر في ذلك، ولذلك لم يكن من الصعب إقناعه، لأنهم كانوا فقراء، وفي حال أن تتزوج زينب فإنه سيصبح من الأسهل إطعام بقية العائلة. ثم إشترى سندباد بيتاً في حي الزهراء، بحيث أنه كان وقتا جيداً للشراء، لأنه كان هناك العديد من الناس المحتاجين، الذين باعوا بيوتهم بثمن رخيص بسبب الحروب. وقبل أن ينتقل إلى المنزل الجديد، طلب سندباد من زينب أن ترافقه في رحلة بحرية لبضعة أيام، لكي يشاركها كنزه العظيم؛ ألا وهو البحر.

ـ أريدك أن تحبي البحر، كما أحبه أنا. قال لها سندباد.

هذه المرة أبحر سندباد وزينب لوحدهما، من دون المساعد. فمنذ اليوم الأول، بدأ سندباد بالنظر إلى زينب برقة، وأكثر ما كان يعجبه بها، عيناها المستديرتين باللون العسلي، وبشرتها الرقيقة الناعمة.... بالتأكيد سيكون لنا أطفال، وآخذهم إلى المدرسة وأعلمهم الإبحار، كان يفكر في هذا سندباد وهو ينظر إلى الأفق البعيد. وبالكاد كان يعرف بعضهما الآخر، فنظرت إليه الفتاة بإرتياب، ربما كانت قلقلة بعض الشيء لأنها لم تكن تعلم أي نوع من الرجال قد تزوجت. فزينب كانت قد تعلمت في المدرسة، وبالطبع كانت تجيد القراءة والكتابة، بالإضافة إلى تدبير أمور المنزل والطهي. وفي ليلة هادئة والقمر كان بدراً، جلسوا على سطح السفينة بالقرب من بعضهما البعض، وأمسكوا بأيدي كل من الاخر، وبدأوا بالحديث عن أسرار الطفولة. وبعد أيام قليلة إكتشفوا الغموض في أجسادهم؛ وأخيراً، وتحت سماءٍ من أشجار النخيل على أحد الشواطئ الفارسية، أصبحوا عشاق. وبعد ثلاثة أسابيع وعندما عادوا إلى البصرة، كانوا قد تغيروا كثيراً، فزينب شعرت بسعادة كبيرة ومن دون خوف، ولديها رغبة كبيرة بأن يستمر سندباد في إخبارها عن المغامرات التي قام بها في

السابق، وكما كان لديها الرغبة في تعليمه القراءة والكتابة، كما كان الاتفاق. وسندباد، الذي عشق البحر لسنين عديدة، الآن، ومع زوجته، فإنه أحب الحياة أكثر فأكثر ولم يريد أي شيء أكثر من ذلك.

وبعد سنة، أنجبت زينب طفلها الأول، كان صبي، وأسموه علي، وسندباد لم يفكر أبداً، بأنه في حال أن يصبح أباً؛ سيكون سعيداً إلى هذا الحد. ولذلك لم يقم بالإبحار بعيداً، وحاول ألا يتأخر كثيراً في العودة إلى بيته، وإذا لم يقم بالتجارة، كان يخرج لصيد الأسماك.

ولكن الفرحة لم تدم طويلا، وبعد فترة وجيزة، بدأ حاكم بلاده حرب أخرى، وقام بغزو الكويت، لكن الإحتلال لهذه البلاد لم يدم إلا لعدة أيام، وذلك لأن عدداً من البلدان، بقيادة أمريكا وبريطانية، أعادوا الإستقلال لهذا البلد. وكانت تلك الأيام، أياماً من الحداد والموت. البصرة، كغيرها من المدن، تعرضت للقصف بقنابل اليورانيوم المُحرم. ولم يكن هناك أي مكان للإحتماء، ودُمرت الغابات الكثيفة بأشجار النخيل على ضفاف شط العرب، وأصبح الساحل حزيناً وعارياً. بعد أسابيع توقفت الهجمات، ولكن ما جاء بعد ذلك كان نوعا مختلفاً من الحروب. المعاناة؛ فمن كان يريد أن يبحث عن الطعام، لم

يجرؤ على الخروج من بيته خوفاً من الطائرات التي كانت تحلق فوق المدينة، كانت المرحلة ما بعد الحرب؛ الحظر.

وفي ذات الوقت، كانت زينب تحمل بطفلها الثاني وكانت مريضة جداً. وكان سندباد بالكاد يقوى على الخروج من المنزل، للبحث عن عمل لإطعام أسرته. وعندما حان وقت الإنجاب، ذهبوا إلى المشفى لأن زينب كانت تعاني كثيراً. وهناك أنجبت زينب فتاة، وأسموها: لطيفة، وقام الأطباء بإجراء العديد من الفحوصات للطيفة، وخاصة سرطان الدم، بحيث أوضحوا أنه منذ إنتهاء الحرب، أنجبَ الكثير من الأطفال مع تشوهات خلقية وأمراض أخرى. كانت لطيفة كالطائر الصغير، بنسمة هواء تطير. وعادوا إلى المنزل، وأمضى سندباد طوال وقته مع زوجته الضعيفة، التي كانت تحاول أن تعتني بطفلتها وترضعها رضاعة طبيعية.

وفي أحد الأيام، وعندما عاد سندباد إلى المنزل بعد البحث عن لقمة العيش، وجد زوجته في حالة الإغماء وشاحبة الوجه، من ذلك المرض الذي بدأ يظهر أثناء الحمل بالطفلة؛ الكوليرا. المرض الذي سيطر على جسدها بالكامل الجسم. وماتت زينب كطائرٌ صغير. وشعر سندباد بوحدة لم يشعر بها من قبل... وبعد الدفن، جلس على ضفة النهر حاضناً علي حتى

عم الظلام. فلم يكن يعرف ماذا يفعل أو إلى أين يذهب! وكان بحاجة إلى أن يعمل لإطعام أطفاله. ولكن، من سيعتني بهم عندما يذهب إلى العمل؟ ترك الأطفال في بيت أحد الجارات لبضعة أيام، التي نصحته بأن يتزوج مرّة أخرى، لأنه بحاجة إلى زوجة لتعتني بالأطفال. ولكن، لم يكن لسندباد الرغبة في الزواج، ولكن الجارة سعت للبحث، ووجدت له فتاة أرملة قُتل زوجها أثناء الحرب، وكان عندها طفلين، الأول عمره سنتين والثاني بضعة أشهر. فتزوجها سندباد، وذهبوا للعيش في منزل سندباد. وهكذا، كان بإمكانها إرضاع لطيفة والإعتناء بالمنزل، وإستطاع سندباد الذهاب إلى صيد الأسماك، والتجارة بالبضائع التي تنقصهم. فلم يتمكن أحد من شرب الماء التي تعرضت للتلوث من اليورانيوم، في حين عانى المزارعين لأن البساتين أصبحت عقيمة، كما أنفسهم! وأشجار النخيل والتين لم تعد تثمر. وكان هذا هو العقاب لمساويء الحاكم.. آه لو أنه لم يكن في هذا البلد سوى حدائق الفاكهة والخضراوات، ولم يكتشفوا هذا النفط اللعين، ربما كنا سنعيش في سلام! كان سندباد يفكر.

وتتوفي لطيفة، الصغيرة والرقيقة، التي لم تستطع مقاومة المرض. وسالت دموع سندباد على خديه حزناً لفراقها، ولكن

سرعان ما جفت تلك الدموع بمرور الزمن. ونادى المؤذن، من مئذنة مسجد الإمام علي -عليه السلام- للصلاة، فرفع سندباد رأسه ونظر إلى السماء.

ومرّت عشر سنوات على تلك الحرب. و خلال ذلك الوقت، كان سندباد وزوجته الجديدة قد اعتادوا على العيش معاً. وكان هم سندباد الوحيد، الحصول على الطعام لعائلته. تاركاً وراءه الأيام السعيدة التى أمضى فيها وقته في الإبحار والبيع والشراء، ولحظات الخوف والحب... ولكنه كان دائماً حاضراً لكل إحتمالات القدر. وغالباً ما كان يبكي فراق زينب، التي تركته ولم ترى علي وهو يكبر، ذلك الفتى الذي عاهدها على أن يعلمه الإبحار، بتلك القدرة الهائلة التي يمتلكها ليكون سعيداً، للعب مع الأطفال في الشارع وفوق الركام وبين الأوساخ أو في المدرسة الباردة والحزينة. هذا هو مستقبل علي.

كان يبدو أنه من غير الممكن أن يحدث أكثر من ذلك، ولكن أمريكا هددت بشن حرب جديدة. والعديد من الناس لم يصدقوا ذلك، ولكن في أحد الأيام كان سندباد في سفينته الشراعية يصيد الأسماك، سمع ضوضاء طائرات، فرفع رأسه وأدرك أنها لم تكن تحلق على النحو المعتاد.

وفي أحد الأيام، وعندما عاد سندباد إلى المنزل بعد البحث عن لقمة العيش، وجد زوجته في حالة الإغماء وشاحبة الوجه.

فهذه المرة كانت أكثر عدداً وأكبر حجماً. وعلى الفور فكر في زوجته وأطفاله في المنزل. فأدار محرك السفينة وعاد مسرعاً نحو المدينة، لكنه فشل في الوصول إلى الميناء لأنه كان مُحتلاً من قبل السفن البريطانية ومئات الجنود، الذين كانوا في كل مكان. فكان عليه أن يهرب وأن يذهب إلى مكان آخر ليرسوا بسفينته، ومن هناك عائداً إلى المنزل سيراً على الأقدام، كان هناك العديد من الجنود والدبابات على الشاطئ، الذين أحاطوا بفندق الشيراتون، والذي إقتحمته الناس اليائسة لسلب كل ما فيه. وفي لحظات قليلة، أصبح الرمز العملاق من الترف العراقي جبلاً من الركام.

عندما وصل سندباد إلى الحي الذي يسكن فيه، وجد حشد كبيراً من الناس! لم يكن يعلم ما الذي حدث، فدخل بين الناس لكي يرى: فوجد أن منزله ومنازل أخرى في الجوار قد دمرت بإحدى الصواريخ. فصرخ صرخة مخيفة وذهب مسرعاً إلى الذي كان منزله، وتمكن من الدخول من خلال إحدى النوافذ، وشق طريقه بين الأنقاض ليعثر على جثث زوجته وأطفالها، وبجانب جثة زوجته وجد إبنه علي وكان لا زال يتنفس، فضمه إلى صدره وخرج به إلى الشارع. وعم الصمت بين الناس، وفي حينها إقتربت مجموعة من الدبابات، فهرع الناس

من المكان وبقي وحده مع إبنه بين ذراعيه. وبدأ سندباد بالمشي إتجاه الدبابات، فأحاطت الدبابات به بشكل دائري في ساحة كانت قائمة من قبل، فرفع جسد علي؛ الجسد المغمور بالدماء، جثة إبنه الحبيب الذي كان يريد أن يبحر معه إلى كل البحار العربية، ليتعرف على أشخاص جدد وبلدان جديدة وليتعلم اللغات والمغامرات والحب والضحك... وسار مع إبنه نحو الدبابات، التي أصبحت أكثر قرباً، لم ير ولم يسمع أحداً ولم يكن لديه شيئ من الدموع. فجأة، توقفت الدبابات، ووصلت سيارة من الصحفيين، وصرخوا على الجنود: لا تلمسوه! لا تلمسوه! ألا ترون أنه يحمل إبنه الميت؟ واستمروا في ذلك إلى أن بدأ الجنود بإطلاق النار على آلآت التصوير.

تلك الصورة التي أنتشرت في أنحاء العالم، ومن ثم، أصبح سندباد معروفاً في جميع أنحاء العالم، ودعت إحدى المنظمات الإنسانية سندباد للذهاب إلى أميركا لشرح حقيقة ما حدث.

لكنه رفض، وهو الذي كان دائماً يحلم بعبور المحيط.

وقال له أحد الصحافيين محاولاً إقناعه:

— إذا ذهبت إلى هناك، فإنك ستظهر على التلفاز وفي الصحف، وسيمكنك أن تشرح ما حدث وأن تقول ما تشاء،

وسار مع إبنه نحو الدبابات، التي أصبحت أكثر قرباً، لم ير
ولم يسمع أحداً.

وربما ستصبح مشهوراً، أو حتى ستبقى لتعيش هناك لأنه لا يوجد لديك مستقبل هنا.

لكنه لم يرى ولم يسمع، فالمستقبل كان قد مات بين ذراعيه. أمريكا موجودة، فمنذ عدة سنوات وأنا أسمع بهذا الإسم، وقد سمعت بما يكفي، فليس من الضروري لأن أذهب إلى مكان ما لأصدق أنه موجود، لأن الدليل كان واضحاً جداً الآن. فقد أخذت أميركا زوجته وإبنته وإبنه، وأخذت زوجته الثانية وأطفالها، وأخذت أميركا الأصدقاء والجيران، وسممت الخس والطماطم في حدائقهم... أمريكا موجودة، لأنهم ومنذ سنوات كانوا قد هاجموا؛ الناس في القرى والحقول، وهم من عزز الحصار، الذى أدى إلى مقتل خمسة آلاف من الأطفال دون سن الخامسة في كل شهر. كنت أعرف أن أمريكا موجودة، فكان هناك أدلة كافية، ولم أرغب بالذهاب إلى هناك.

— أنا من هنا، في المدينة التي شهدت على ولادتي وشبابي، حيث كنت سعيداً، حيث وجدت الحب. هذا هو بيتي، مدمر، ملوث ومليء بالدخان. لم يتبقى لي شيئاً: لا سفينة ولا منزل ولا عائلة ولا أمل. ولا حتى الدمع، فلم يبقى لي منه شيئاً. ولكنني ما زلت إنسان.

ولم يكن لسندباد مدافع ولا صواريخ ولا قنابل ولا دبابات، ولكن لديه يدين وقدمين إثنتين، ومع كل ذلك دماغاً، ما زال يمكنه أن يفكر. جالساً أمام تلك المياه التي أحب، وقرر أنه لن يدوس على كرامته أحد. ونهض، وأخذ حجراً ووضعه في جيبه، وسار بحزم ودون خوف؛ حجراً مستديراً من على الشاطئ، وضغط عليه بشدّة. البصرة كانت مدينته وبيته، ولن يخرجه أحد منها، والحجر الذي منحه القوة عندما كان يلامسه بيده، فالبصرة هي التي مثلت بحره ومدينته وثقافته ومساجدهم، ومثلت الناس الذين أحبها سندباد. في كل مرة كان يمشي بسرعة أكبر، متجاهلاً مخاطر الحرب. وعندما وصل إلى مركز مدينة البصرة، كأنها كانت الصحوة: أدار رأسه ورأى العديد من الرجال والنساء والفتيان، الذين كانوا مثله، كل واحد منهم يحمل حجراً في يده. وساروا معاً، بصمتٍ وبعزم، ورؤوسهم مرفوعة عالياً، وفي كل لحظة كان عددهم يزداد وكانوا يشعرون بقوة أكبر. فكان لديهم ما يحتاجون لينتصروا؛ الحق. فمن الممكن أن يستغرق ذلك وقتاً... ولكنه حتماً آتي.

وفي يوم من الأيام سيعودوا للإبحار ويصبحوا سعداء.

الشعب العراقي قد إنتصر.
ولذلك إجتثوا سواعد أطفالهم:
فإذا كانوا قد إنتصروا،
فعلى الأقل لن يستطيعوا الإشارة بعلامة النصر بأصابعهم.

سانتياغو ألبا ريكو

علي بابا

جلوريا أريمون

بالتعاون مع يوسف لورمان

كان علي بابا متزوجاً من إمرأة فقيرة، إسمها مرجانة، وكانوا يعانون من مصاعب مالية كثيرة. وكان علي بابا يذهب في كل يوم إلى الغابة لجمع الحطب وبعض الأعشاب، وأيضاً لجمع بعض التمر والكستناء، كلٌ في موسمه، وبعد ذلك، كان يبيع كل ما كان يجمع في السوق. أما أخوه قاسم، فكان متزوجاً من إمرأة ثرية، وكان تاجراً، وكان لديه مقدرة فطرية لزيادة ثراءه وممتلكاته. فكان يشتري البضائع بأثمانٍ زهيدة، ويحتكرها ومن ثم يبيعها بأثمانٍ عالية، ليس لديه ذمة ولا أخلاق، فكان يشتري بضائع مسروقة أو مهربة من البلدان المجاورة، مثل: المواد الغذائية، والآلات، والنفط، والأدوية...إلخ. وكان يبيع

هذه البضائع من خلال مجموعة من التجار الفاسدين. فكان همه الوحيد جمع المزيد من الأموال، في حين أن التجارة قد تقلصت كثيراً بسبب الإحتلال الأمريكي، ومع ذلك فإن تجارته كانت تسير على ما يرام، فكان يبيع البضائع للمُحتلين وللمقاومة في الوقت ذاته.

وفي أحد الأيام، عندما كان علي بابا يعمل في الغابة، شاهد عدداً كبيراً من المركبات، وكان الغبار يتطاير من حولها، فخاف وأختبأ في كهف قريب؛ ففي حال أنهم كانوا الأمريكيون فإنهم سيلقون القبض عليه، مع أنه لم يكن يفعل شيئا سوى أنه كان يجمع الحطب كالعادة، فلربما يقبضون عليه لذلك!

ومن مكان مظلم في داخل الكهف، حبس علي بابا أنفاسه لكي لا يكتشفوا وجوده، كما إستطاع أن يرى، أنهم في الواقع كانوا جنوداً أمريكيون، وبدأوا بإدخال صناديق مليئة بالأسلحة في الكهف حيث كان مختبأ، وأخفوا الصناديق داخل حجرة في داخل الكهف ذاته. في البداية، تعجب علي بابا، ومن ثم فكر.. إنه من المؤكد مستودع لتخزين الأسلحة، ففي حال هاجمت المقاومة معسكرات الجنود المعروفة، فإنهم لن يدمروا مخزون الذخيرة لديهم.. حقاً، إن هؤلاء الأمريكيين أذكياء.

وعندما إنتهوا من إدخال كل الصناديق، قام أحد الجنود بإدخال

...إستطاع أن يرى، أنهم في الواقع كانوا جنوداً أمريكييون، وبدأوا بإدخال صناديق مليئة بالأسلحة في الكهف حيث كان مختبأ، وأخفوا الصناديق داخل حجرة في داخل الكهف ذاته.

رقم سري على لوحة المفاتيح المخبأة على أحد جدران الكهف، ومن ثم أغلقت البوابة كما كانت قد فُتحت، ووضع الجندي الورقة التي كان مكتوب عليها رمز العبور للبوابة في جيبه، وكان الأخير في الخروج من الكهف، وأثناء خروجه، سحب منديلاً من جيبه ليجفف عرق وجهه. ومن ثم أعاده إلى جيبه، وغادر الكهف من دون أن يدرك أنه أسقط الورقة التي تحوي رمز العبور للبوابة. أثناء ذلك، لم تغب أعين علي بابا عن الجندي ولا للحظة واحدة، وظل مختبئاً إلى أن سمع أصوات محركات العربات وهي تدور وتتجه بعيداً، فخرج من مكان إختباءه وذهب مباشرة إلى حيث سقطت الورقة. أخذها ونظر إليها، وكانت عبارة عن مزيج من عشرة أرقام وأحرف، وبخجل، قام بالضغط على لوحة المفاتيح المخبأة على جدار الكهف، تماماً كمام فعل الجنود، فُتحت البوابة، دُهل بما رأت عيناه؛ رأى العشرات والعشرات من الصناديق المكدسة بالأسلحة.

هيّا!!! فهذه ترسانة حقيقية! كان يتمتم. وعلى الفور فكر في الإستيلاء على إحدى الأسلحة للدفاع عن عائلته. ففي الحي الذي يعيش فيه، ويوماً من بعد يوم، تأتي فرق من الجنود ويقتحموا البيوت فجأة، ويفتشوا فيها ويعتقلوا أهلها بحجة

البحث عن الإرهابيين.؛ فعاد إلى بيوتهم عدد قليل من الذين قاموا بأسرهم، وفي حال أنهم عادوا، فإنهم كانوا في حالة يرثى لها، في حين أن الناس فضلت موتهم على رؤيتهم على هذا الحال.

ومن ناحية أخرى، كان من الخطير جداً إمتلاك سلاحاً في المنزل... لم يعرف ماذا يفعل، ولكن في نهاية المطاف ومع رغبته في ضمان سلامة عائلته، أخذ بندقية نصف أوتوماتيكية وعلبة من الرصاص. ومن ثم أدخل رمز العبور مرّة أخرى، فأغلقت البوابة وعاد إلى منزله.

كان علي بابا منفعلاً جداً، فأخبر زوجته بما كان قد إكتشف. وقرر الإثنان إخفاء البندقية في مكان سري داخل المنزل، وفي الوقت ذاته، يمكن الوصول إليها بسرعة، في حال داهم الجنود منزلهم في الليل. وبينما كانوا يتكلمون في أمر البندقية، لم يدركوا أن إبنهم الصغير أحمد، كان في الغرفة المجاورة وسمع كل شيء.

في اليوم التالي، أحمد، الذي كان يذهب للعب كل مساء مع ابن عمه، في منزل العم قاسم، قال: الآن لن يمكن أن يحدث لنا أي مكروه، لأن أبي لديه بندقية جيدة جداً، والتي عثر عليها في أحد الكهوف، إذا هاجمنا الجنود في الليل، فإننا سنقتلهم!

وعندما سمع قاسم بذلك، فتح عينيه الإثنتين إلى أقصى حدٍ وفكر: هممم، الأسلحة، دائماً كانت تجارتها رابحة! وكان يريد أن يعرف من أين حصل أخوه على البندقية.

وفي مساء ذات اليوم، ذهب قاسم لرؤية علي بابا، وسأله عن البندقية وكيف حصل عليها؟. فأخبره علي بابا عن إكتشافه. ومن ثم..، قاسم، الذي إمتلكه الطمع والجشع، إقترح أن يسرق كل الأسلحة ويبيعها بأفضل ثمن، سواءً كان داخل البلاد أو خارجها.

— ففي أفغانستان، فإنهم سيدفعون أموالاً كثيرة مقابل هذه الأسلحة، — قالها: وهو متحمس.

— ماذا؟ هل أنت مجنون؟ إن الذي تقترحه أمر خطير جداً، ماذا سيفعل الأمريكيين عندما يجدوا الكهف فارغاً؟

— أجابه قاسم: عندما يكتشفوا ذلك، نكون قد صرنا من الأغنياء وبعيدين عن هنا.

تجادل الأخوين وقت طويلا، إلى أن هدّد قاسم أخاه، بأنه سيخبر الأمريكيين عن أمره في حال لم يوافق على العمل معه في تجارة الأسلحة. وفكر علي بابا بالذي قاله أخاه، بحيث أنه أقدم على فعل أمور مشابه من قبل، وهو يعلم أن اخاه يفضل المال على أي شيء آخر.

جثة داخل تابوت. حفرة في المقبرة، ورأس متجه نحو مكة
المكرمة. حزنٌ ودموع.

فكيف يمكن أن يكون هناك أناس مساكين إلى هذا الحد في العالم!؟ أنجبتهم ذات الأم، ورضعوا ذات الحليب وتعلموا في ذات المدرسة... كيف من الممكن إذاً أن يكونوا مختلفين إلى هذا الحد؟

– ألا تعتقد أنه في حال وافقتك الرأي، سنكون كلنا في خطر، ليس أنا وأنت فقط. ألا تهمك عائلتك؟ – مجيباً علي بابا أخاه. فاستشاط قاسم غضباً بسبب عناد شقيقه، واقترب منه وأمسك برقبته.

– أرى أمامي أكبر صفقة تجارية في حياتي، وأنت لن تمنعني من القيام بها. فإما أن تخبرني عن مكان الكهف أو أقسم بأنني سأذهب مباشرة إلى معسكر الأمريكيين في حال خروجي من هذا المنزل.

وإرتعد جسد علي بابا. فأخوه كان قادراً على فعل ذلك وأكثر. لذلك، أخبره عن مكان الكهف ومستودع الأسلحة، وأعطاه ورقة رمز العبور للدخول والخروج. وأفعل ما أنت فاعل، ولم يرد أن يسمع شيئا آخر من أخيه.

وفي صباح اليوم التالي، أخذ قاسم شاحنته وذهب إلى الكهف مسرعاً، وأدخل رمز العبور، إنفتحت البوابة ودخل إلى مستودع الأسلحة، ولكي لا يراه أحد وهو في داخل

المستودع، قام بإدخال رمز العبور من اللوحة الموجودة في الداخل، فأغلقت البوابة من جديد. "آه، يا حبيب النبي"! عندما رأى كل تلك الصناديق المكدسة، التي تحتوي على كل شيء، وكان متحمساً جداً. فهذه وتلك، تباع في السوق السوداء بأسعار كبيرة! وعندها سأصبح من الأغنياء إلى الأبد، وعندما سأقوم ببيع كل الصناديق، سأذهب أنا وعائلتي إلى بلدٍ آخر، وحينها، يمكن للأمريكيين أن يبحثوا عني؛ فلقد سئم من سنوات الحرب الطويلة، فيذهب هو وعائلته إلى مكان فيه فرص عمل جيدة لتاجر مثلي... لدولة ناشئة. الصين، على سبيل المثال. هنالك الكثير من الفرص في العالم!.

ومن دون إضاعة للوقت، وضع قاسم بعض الصناديق بالقرب البوابة، ليضعها لاحقاً في شاحنته. وعندما حان الوقت لمغادرة الكهف، وضع يده في جيبه لسحب ورقة رمز العبور. لكنه لم يجدها!!!

– اللعنة، أين قمت بوضع هذه الورقة؟ "تمتم بعصبية، بينما كان يبحث في جيوبه الأخرى". من المؤكد أنها سقطت على الأرض، بينما كنت أقوم بجر الصناديق... إهدأ، إهدأ، فلا بد أن أجدها.

وبحث في كل شبر من الارض حيث كان قد ذهب، ولكنه لم

يعثر على الورقة. وظل يبحث ويبحث، وأمضى وقت طويل وهو ويبحث.. إلى أن يأس من العثور عليها، فبدأ يجرب بعض الرموز التي بدت إليه أنه كان قد ضغط عليها قبلاً: DX450MA789. لم يحدث شيئاً. DZ450MA739. لا شيء! JX450ME789. لا شيء أيضاً!! فلم تنفتح البوابة، وفي كل مرة كان يشعر بتوتر أكثر وأكثر. وكما كان سميناً، فإنه كان يتصبب عرقاً مثل الثور الهائج. "يجب أن أخرج، يجب أن أخرج" كان يكررها لتشجيع نفسه. ولكن لم يتغير شيء، فلم يكن لديه حل. وبدأ يشعر بدوران في رأسه، وأحس أنه سمع صوت طنين. في النهاية، أدرك أنه لم يكن مجرد طنين داخل رأسه، بحيث سمع وأحس بهذا الطنين وكان يأتي من الخارج... طنين شبيه بأصوات المحركات... نعم، كانت أصوات محركات، وكانت تقترب... ومن ثم توقفت!

وهنا، دخل قاسم في دوامة من الأفكار من شدة الخوف، وتذكر كل تحذيرات أخيه، ولم يكن لديه وقت إلا ليختبئ خلف بعض الصناديق آملاً بأن ينجوا. ولكنه لم يفلح، لأن الجنود كانوا قد اكتشفوا شاحنته في الخارج، وعثروا عليه خلال دقائق معدودة.

وفي ذات الوقت، زوجته فاطمة: تأخر قاسم عن عادته في

العودة إلى المنزل! وبدأت تشعر بالقلق. فهي كانت تعلم إلى أين كان قد ذهب، ومرت الساعات، وكان القلق يزداد. في النهاية، ذهبت إلى علي بابا.

وعند حلول الظلام، ذهب علي بابا إلى الكهف ووجد جثة أخيه على مدخل الكهف، ممزقة ومغطاة بالدماء، وكان أحد الضباع قد قطع أجزاء من جسده. وشاحنة أخيه لم تكن هناك. حملَ الجثة، وعاد بها متخفياً إلى المنزل. ماذا سأفعل الآن؟

– فلم أجروء على دفنه هناك، خوفاً من أن يعود الجنود أثناء ذلك، – قال لزوجته. ومن ناحيه أخرى، أن يجلب الجثة إلى المنزل سيكون أسوأ، وبدأت فاطمة بالصراخ والبكاء، ويسمع صراخها الجيران... ماذا سنفعل الآن؟ ماذا سنفعل؟.

مورجانه، بالإضافة إلى أنها كانت جميلة، فكانت ذكية جداً، وعلى الفور وجدت حلاً. فإقترحت وضع الجثة داخل حقيبة كبيرة في فناء المنزل، تحت كومة من الأثاث القديم. وكانوا في فصل الشتاء؛ فيمكن للجثة أن تصمد بعض الأيام. ففعلوا ذلك، وحينها طلبت مرجانه من زوجها أن يذهب إلى الشرطة، ليبلغ عن أن أحد اللصوص قد سرق شاحنة أخيه.

– وفي حال سألوك، ولماذا لم يأتي هو للإبلاغ عن السرقة؟ أخبرهم بأنه مريض جداً.

وفي صباح اليوم التالي، ذهبت مرجانه إلى بيت الطبيب، وقالت له: هل لك أن تعطيني بعض الأدوية لشقيق زوجي؟ فهو مريض جداً. ولذلك قمنا بإحضاره إلى منزلنا، فزوجته لا تستطيع الإعتناء به وحدها.

أعطها الطبيب دواءً لآلام البطن والمعدة، كما أخبرته مرجانه عن حالته، وفي اليوم التالي، عادت مرجانه مرّة أخرى إلى الطبيب، وقالت له: إن حالته أصبحت أسوأ من الأمس. وفي اليوم الثالث قالوا إن قاسم قد توفى، ولم يستغرب أحداً من موته. فعلى أي حال، كان الموت شيئاً طبيعياً منذ أن بدأ الغزو. وطوال تلك الأيام لم تخرج زوجة قاسم من المنزل لكي لا يكتشف الناس الخدعة، ومن ثم أعلنت عائلة قاسم عن الجنازة والعزاء، وبدا كل شيء طبيعي. جثة داخل تابوت. حفرة في المقبرة، ورأس متجه نحو مكة المكرمة. حزنٌ ودموع. تعازي الأصدقاء والجيران. قهوة وبعض الحلويات لشكر الناس على المساندة. ولكن المشكلة كانت في كيفية التخلص من جثة قاسم التي قد بدأت تحلل. وفي الواقع كان هناك مشكلة أخرى.

فالأمريكيون كانوا في حيرة من أمرهم، وكانوا يريدون معرفة هوية الشخص الذي كان داخل الكهف.

خرج قطيع الحمير من مركز الشرطة، وقطعوا جزءاً كبيراً
من المدينة، إلى أن وصلوا أمام منزل علي بابا.

فكما كان يحدث أحياناً، أطلق الجنود النار على قاسم ومن ثم قاموا بإستجوابه. ولكن تلك الطلقات كانت قد أصابته بجروح بالغة، بحيث أنه لم يكن قادراً على الإجابة عن أي من الأسئلة التي طرحوها: من أنت؟ كيف تمكنت من الدخول إلى المستودع؟ هل أعطاك أحد ما رمز العبور؟ وإذا كان كذلك، كم شخصاً يعرف بهذا المستودع؟ ومن هم؟.

وكإجراء إحترازي، نقل الأمريكيون الأسلحة من الكهف إلى مخبأ آخر. ومن ثم بدأوا بالتحقيق لكشف هوية مالك الشاحنة.

بسبب حالة الفوضى الإدارية في بغداد، استغرق الكشف عن هوية مالك الشاحنة مدة أسبوع، وكان مالكها تاجر يدعى قاسم، الذي كان قد دفن قبل ثلاثة أيام بسبب المرض.

– بحال أنه كان مريضاً جداً، فماذا كانت تفعل شاحنته على مدخل الكهف؟ – سأل المحقق فهد "من الشرطة العراقية" علي بابا.

– في الواقع، سرق أحد اللصوص الشاحنة في مساء ذالك اليوم. – أجاب علي بابا بكل هدوء ممكن، وأظهر له ورقة إدعاء السرقة.

فلم يبقى شيئاً يقوله. لكن المحقق لم يقتنع، وأحس أن هناك شيء مريب جداً. وهكذا قال الأمريكيون أيضاً.

لم يكن لديهم أي دليل على أن علي بابا كان يعرف شيئاً عن الكهف، كما أنهم كانوا يعرفون أيضاً أن علي بابا لم يكن يعمل بالتجارة مع أخاه. ولكنه كان مشتبهاً به، ولم يريدوا أن يخاطروا في الحكم. فكان عليهم أن يعتقلوهم جميعاً، هو وعائلته للتحقيق معهم.

ولكن، علي بابا كان محبوباً ومعروفاً جيداً لأهل القرية، فمن الممكن أن يسبب إعتقاله بعض المشاكل. فأوصى المحقق فهد أن يتم إعتقاله سراً، وبأقصى حد ممكن من الهدوء. وعرض عليهم خطته، وكانت كما لو أنها أخذت من حكايات ألف ليلة وليلة.

ألا تعتقدون أن هنالك الكثير من تجار الزيت؟ ألم تروا أن العديد منهم، وبسبب الصعوبات للحصول على البنزين، قد عادوا إلى الطرق القديمة في إستخدام الحمير لنقل البضائع؟ أليس ذلك صحيحاً؟ – معلقاً المحقق فهد، ويريد أن يظهر جدارته أمام الامريكيون. فسوف نتخفى أنا ورجالي بلباس ومعدات تجار الزيت، وسوف نحضر لكم علي بابا وزوجته وأولاده الأربعة من دون أن يشعر أحد بذلك.

فضحك الأمريكيون على خطة فهد، ولكنهم وافقوا عليها. ففي حال أنه فعل ما قال، فسوف يزوده الأمريكيون بالشوكولاته،

طوال الوقت الذي سيمكث فيه الامريكيين. كان فهد يحب الشوكولاته كثيراً.

إشترى المحقق فهد ثمانية جرار كبيرة، وحمّلها على أربعة حمير، وكان يتظاهر بأنها مليئة بالزيت. في الواقع، كان هناك جرتان فقط مملوءة بالزيت. أما الجرار الأخرى فقد إختبأ بداخلها ستة رجال من الشرطة. خرج قطيع الحمير من مركز الشرطة، وقطعوا جزءً كبيراً من المدينة إلى أن وصلوا أمام منزل علي بابا، وكانت الشمس قد غربت وبدأ البرد يشتد. المحقق فهد، متقمصاً شخصية بائع زيت، طرق باب المنزل وقال لعلي بابا، أنه كان صديق قديم لأخيه قاسم، كان قد تعرف عليه من خلال التجارة؛ وكان قد ذهب إلى منزله، ولكن قبل أن يطرق الباب، أخبره بعض الجيران بأنه قد توفى وأن عائلته تعاني كثيراً لفقدانه. ولذلك طلب منه المبيت تلك الليلة لأنه لم يرد أن يزعج عائلة المتوفى. وأن الوقت قد تأخر ويجب عليه أن يكمل طريقه إلى الكاظمية في صباح اليوم التالي ليبيع الزيت.

ـ فأنا لا أثق بالشرطة، كما تعلم. قالها فهد محاولاً إقناعه، فإذا قمت بترك الحمير في الشارع فإنني أخاف أن يستولوا على البضاعة. فأنت تعلم كم هو من الصعب الحصول على

الزيت في هذه الأيام. وبالنسبة إلي، فإنه يعني كل شيء، فزوجتي وأولادي السبعة ينتظرونني في المنزل، لأعود إليهم بالنقود من بيع الزيت وأوفر لهم الطعام. ولإيضاح كلماته، أخذ إبريق الكيل، وملئه بالزيت. وقال: لحسن ضيافتك لي، فإنني سأملئ جرة المطبخ عندك بالزيت.

ومن بعد كل هذه العبارات، إقتنع علي بابا على إستضافة التاجر في منزله، وأدخله إلى فناء المنزل، وأتجه إلى الإسطبل ليدخل الحمير والزيت، وبعد أن إنتهوا من ذلك، دعا علي بابا التاجر إلى بيته.

ـ رباه، لا لا، لا أريد أن أزعجكم، فأنا أفضل بالبقاء هنا في الإسطبل، مع الحمير. لا تقلقوا بشأني فأنا تعب جداً وسأخلد إلى النوم في غضون ثوان.

تعجب علي بابا كثيراً لأن التاجر رفض دعوته، ولكنه لم يلح عليه كثيراً بالدخول إلى المنزل معتقداً أنه يفضل البقاء بالقرب من بضاعته الثمينة ليراقبها.

فدخل علي بابا إلى المنزل وأخبر زوجته مرجانه بكل ما حصل، وكانت في المطبخ تحضر الطعام، وأظهرت الزوجه بأنها كانت راضية عن القرار الذي إتخذه زوجها لإستضافة التاجر.

ولكي لا يظهر كالأحمق، ولكي ينسى الأمريكيون أمر علي بابا وعائلته، قال للأمريكيون أنه قد تعقدت الأمور بعض الشيء، ولذلك كان من الواجب قتلهم جميعاً.

- وقالت الزوجة: عندما أنتهي من الطبخ، سأقدم بعض الحساء للتاجر؛ بحيث منع علي بابا أولاده الذهاب إلى الإسطبل لكي لا يضايقوا على التاجر. وبعدها خرج علي بابا في مأمورية.

- لا تتأخر كثيراً فالعشاء على وشك أن يجهز، قالت له زوجته ذلك عندما رأته يغادر المنزل.

وعندما إنتهت من الطبخ، حضرت وعاء من الحساء وذهبت لتقديمه إلى التاجر، ولكن عندما إقتربت من الباب، سمعت بأشخاص يهمسون. فاقتربت ببطء وحذر.

- سمعت صوت رجل يتمتم: ننتظر إلى أن يخلد جميعهم إلى النوم لنقوم بعملنا.

- ولكنه ليس مريحاً على الإطلاق المكوث داخل الجِرار؛ كان يشتكي أحد الشرطة المختبئين للمحقق.

- هششششش! هدوء، هدوء، هل تريد أن يكنشفوا أمرنا؟

بهذا إكتفت مرجانه لتكون متأكدة بالذي كان يحدث. فذلك الرجل لم يكن تاجراً، وإنما كان شخصاً ينوي خطفهم تلك الليلة، وليصبحوا في رحمة الله! ماذا كان عليهم أن يفعلوا؟؟ فتلك الحادثة أعادت إلى ذاكرة مرجانه القصة المشهورة للأربعين حرامي اللذين إختبئوا داخل الجِرار.

– إذًا، سأفعل كما فعل بطل القصة! وسأجعلهم يقعون في المصيدة! قالت ذلك من بعد أن سيطرت على خوفها.

وبهدوء تام، عادت إلى المطبخ، وبدلاً من وعاء الحساء، أعدت طبق كبير من الطعام، ووضعت في الطبق، كل الطعام الذي كان موجوداً لعشاء العائلة في ذلك المساء. ومن ثم ذهبت وأحضرت مخدراً؛ الذي كانت تستخدمه كمهدء ومخفف للآلام، وقامت بوضع جرعات صغيرة في الطعام. ومع هذا الطبق الكبير والشهي ذهبت إلى الإسطبل، ولكن قبل أن تقترب أصدرت بعض الضجة لكي يسمعوا وصولها.

– أيها التاجر! لقد أحضرت لك القليل من الطعام للعشاء، هل يمكنني الدخول؟

سمعت صوت خطوات سريعة؛ بحيث عاد الثعالب إلى مخابئهم.

– نعم نعم، لحظة واحدة... إنني أبدل ملابسي...

كان عذراً بطبيعة الحال، فمن سيبدل ملابسه لينام داخل إسطبل شديد البرودة؟

– يمكنك الدخول، قال التاجر المزعوم.

دخلت مرجانه حاملة الطبق، وعندما رأى المحقق فهد، الطبق الذي قدمته إليه، نظر إليها مذهولاً من كرم هؤلاء الناس.

— إلى أين أنت ذاهبة أيتها السيدة بكل هذا الطعام؟ هذا طعام لعشرة أشخاص!!

— قال لي زوجي بأنك تعب جداً، وغداً في الصباح الباكر ستسافر إلى الكاظمية، والتي تبعد عشرون كيلومتراً عن هنا. فعليك أن تأكل جيداً لتقوى على السفر.

— ولكن هذا كثير جداً.

— في منزلنا، نحب أن نعامل الضيوف كما لو أنهم كانوا أمراء. ونشعر بالفخر بالقيام بذلك، ويجب أن لا تدع شيئاً من الطعام، لأننا في هذا الحال سنكون مستائين جداً.

— لا شيء في نيتي أبعد من الإساءة إليكم. قالها المحتال مع قليل من الندم.

— هنيئاً لك الطعام وأحلاماً سعيدة. غداً سأعود لآخذ الصحون والطبق.

خرجت مرجانه وأغلقت باب الإسطبل، وكلها أمل أن يسير كل شيء كما هو مخطط له.

جاء علي بابا، وأخبرته زوجته بالذي إكنشفته عن التاجر المحتال، وعن الذي قامت بفعله. فإذا سار كل شيء كما هو مخطط له، وتقاسم التاجر المحتال الطعام مع رجاله، فإنه وبعد وقت قصير سوف ينامون كلهم نوماً عميقاً، وتفر العائلة.

الهروب، بالمساعدة القيمة للحمير الأربعة في نقل أثاث المنزل.

وهكذا حدث. في الواقع، شارك المحقق فهد العشاء مع رجاله، تماماً كما تصورت مرجانه، وغط كل الرجال في نوم عميق، حتى أنهم لم يسمعوا أي من الأصوات عند فرار عائلة علي بابا من المنزل، وبحيث أنهم أخرجوا الحمير من الإسطبل وإستخدموها للفرار مع أثاث المنزل. ومن جديد، أنقظ ذكاء مرجانه العائلة من أزمة حرجة.

وفي اليوم التالي، وعندما إستيقظ المحقق فهد ورجاله، وجدوا المنزل فارغاً، وعثروا على رسالة مكتوب فيها: "بصحة وعافية!!".

وشعر المحقق بأنه قد خدع، فغضب جداً، ولكنه كل ما فكر بما حدث، كان يهدأ مثمناً ذكاء تلك السيدة. إلى أن بدا له الأمر مضحكاً. كان يستحق ما حصل له، لأنه أراد إيذاء الفقراء. ولكي لا يظهر كالأحمق، ولكي ينسى الأمريكيون أمر علي بابا وعائلته، قال للأمريكيون أنه قد تعقدت الأمور بعض الشيء، ولذلك كان من الواجب عليهم قتلهم جميعاً؛ وأنهم أجهزوا عليهم جميعاً ولم يشعر بهم أحد من الجيران.

ومن بعد هذه الكذبة، التي تقاسمها هو ورجاله، الذين لم يريدون أن يظهروا كالحمقى أيضاً. وهدأت مخاوف المحقق فهد، وكان ضميره راضياً تماما. ولكن ليس هناك شوكولاته،

قال الأمريكيين."لأن قتلهم لم يكن ضمن الإتفاق" فأجاب "إلا بوجود أسباب قاهرة". الجملة التي سمعهم يرددونها كثيراً.

مع مرور الزمن. هرمَ علي بابا ومرجانه، وعاشوا حياة رديئة، ولكن بهدوء، في الأردن. إلى أن جاءتهم المنية، ليجدوا السلام في الآخرة، لأنهم أوفوا بتعاليم دينهم، ولم يؤذوا أحداً، وحرصوا دائماً على مساعدة المحتاجين.

مصباح علاء الدين السحري

كان علاء الدين صبياً من أسرة بسيطة، كان في الثانية عشرة من عمرة وكان محب للحياة، فقد توفى والده في الحرب، وكانت والدته تعمل في حياكة الملابس لدى أحد الخياطين. كانوا يعيشون في حي الرصافة؛ في الحي القديم لبغداد وبالقرب من نهر دجلة. المدرسة التي كان يذهب إليها، كانت قديمة وباردة، وكانت جدرانها عارية، ولكنها لم تخلوا يوماً من الصورة الكبيرة للرئيس، وكان هناك بعض النوافذ المكسرة، والتي لم يقم أحداً بتغييرها منذ عدة أشهر. والمعلمة، كانت إمرأة طويلة القامة وسمينة، وعلى الرغم من مشاكسة الطلاب، فإنها وفي كثير من الأحيان لم تكن توبخهم على ذلك. وكانت دائماً تبدو متعبة، ولكن علاء الدين والطلاب الآخرين

لم يفهموا لماذا هي كذلك! فعلى العكس فهم لديهم الرغبة في الجري والقفز واللعب! وفي أحد المرّات، تغيب أحد الطلاب عن المدرسة، ولكنه ومنذ ذلك اليوم، لم يعد إلى المدرسة مرة أخرى! ومن ثم، ومن دون وعي عن الذي قد حصل، توقف اللعب وإمتلئت النظرات بظلام داكن السواد. سأل علاء الدين والدته عن السبب الذي جعل ذلك الصبي يتوقف فجأة عن الذهاب الى المدرسة؟!، وكان دائما يحصل على نفس الإجابة: "لقد مات من الجوع، الخوف أو الحزن". ولأيام قليلة، كان علاء الدين صامتاً وحزيناً، ولكن سرعان ما عادت إليه الرغبة في القفز واللعب.

أحياناً، عندما كان يخرج الطلاب من المدرسة، كانت تذهب مجموعة من الأطفال إلى المستنصرية؛ التي كانت في فترة العباسيين، عبارة عن مكان إقامة لسلالة قديمة من الخلفاء اللذين قطنوا بغداد، وكان هناك إحدى أهم الجامعات، والتي كان يدرّس فيها، الأكثر تقدماً في علم الفلك والصيدلة والطب. كانوا يتسللون إلى الفناء المركزي ويختلسون النظر من خلال نوافذ الفصول الدراسية.

المدرسة التي كان يذهب إليها، كانت قديمة وباردة، وكانت جدرانها عارية، ولكنها لم تخلوا يوماً من الصورة الكبيرة للرئيس، وكان هناك بعض النوافذ المكسرة، والتي لم يقم أحداً بتغييرها منذ عدة أشهر.

كثيراً من الأحيان ومن بعد الظهيرة، كان علاء الدين وأصدقائه يصعدون على سطح المدرسة، ويقضون وقتاً طويلاً في التأمل والنظر إلى النهر. بحيث كان يقسم نهر دجلة المدينة إلى قسمين، وكان هناك عشر جسور للعبور من جانب إلى آخر، والتي كانت دائماً مزدحمة بالسيارات والشاحنات والدراجات والعربات... تلك الجسور التي دمرتها الحروب مراراً وتكراراً، والتي وفي كل مرّة، كان يعيد بناؤها سكان بغداد الصامدون. ومن هناك، كان غروب الشمس يغمر أسطح المنازل ومآذن المساجد باللون الأحمر. وفي إحدى الليالي ومن دون أن يدركوا، تأخر الوقت ونزل الليل وهم جالسون هناك، وعادوا إلى منازلهم من بعد منتصف الليل؛ وكانت أمهاتهم قد قلقن عليهم كثيراً بسبب تأخرهم.

ــ لقد سبق لي أن قلت لك ألف مرة، أنني لا أريدك أن تدور في الشوارع إلى هذا الوقت، صرخت والدة علاء الدين، في الوقت الذي خفض علاء الدين عينيه، تائباً.

بالإضافة إلى الساعات التي كان يقضيها في المدرسة، كان علاء الدين يحب الذهاب إلى السوق، حيث كان يملأ أجيابه بفائض الفواكه والخضروات. وكان دائماً يراقب العمال والتجار؛ الحداد الذي يطاوع قطع الحديد أو الإسكافي الذي

يرقع الأحذية أو الكاتب الذي يكتب الرسائل للأشخاص اللذين لا يعرفون الكتابة. فهو كان يريد أن يتعلم الكثير في المدرسة، لكي يستطيع كتابة الرسائل لمن يشاء.

في المساء، وبعد تناول العشاء المعتاد مع والدته، كان يذهب علاء الدين ليتمشى على ضفة نهر دجلة، وكان يراقب المطاعم وهم يقومون بشوي الأسماك. ومن ثم كان يذهب إلى شارع أبو نواس، من على جسر الجمهورية إلى جسر بغداد المعلق (14 تموز)؛ فقد كانت هذه أسماء بعض الجسور من عهد صدام، وما زالوا يسمونها هكذا. لم يأكل شيئاً من تلك الأسماك، ولكن الرائحة كانت تعطيه متعة خاصة؛ فكان يفتح أنفه إلى أقصى حد، ويتنفس بعمق، إلى أن تصل الرائحة تقريباً إلى معدته، وهكذا كان يشعر بسعادة. ومن ثم كان يسير إلى أن يصل إلى الميناء، حيث كان هناك نصب تذكاري لشهرزاد، بطلة حكايات ألف ليلة وليلة.

في إحدى الليالي، بالقرب من المياه، بينما كان يراقب أحد الصيادين، رأى شيئاً يلمع في الماء، فاقترب بحذر وأخذه، وعندما خرج من الماء أدرك أنه كان مصباحاً، لم يكن كبيراً وكان مصنوعاً من النحاس. وتذكر القصة التي كانت تقصها عليه والدته عندما كان صغيراً لينام. "الآن، لا يوجد جان"،

قال علاء الدين. ولكنه لم يستطع أن يقاوم رغبته، ففرك المصباح بلطف، ومن ثم بقوة أكبر. وفكر "على الاقل سيكون لامعاً أكثر، قبل أن أذهب إلى المنزل وأهديه لأمي". ولكنه كاد أن يموت من شدة الخوف عندما، فجأة بدأ المصباح بإصدار ضجيج من الداخل، وكأن بداخله ماء يغلي، ومن ثم إنطلق من المصباح دخان كثيف إلى أن، وفي النهاية، خرج له جني المصباح. "هذا ليس حقيقياً، فهذا يحدث في القصص فقط!" ثم فرك علاء الدين عينيه، وقرص خديه، ليتأكد من أنه كان مستيقظاً وأنه لا يحلم، وشاهد بدهشة الجني، الذي ظل جالساً أمامه.

— سيدي، قال له الشيء الغريب في حين كان ينحني برأسه، أشكرك على إخراجي من الظلمة. فلم أخرج من المصباح منذ مئات السنين!

— هل أنت حقاً جني المصباح أم أنني أحلم؟ سأله علاء الدين، وكان ما يزال خائفاً بعض الشيء. لا، أجابه الجني، إنه ليس حلماً، فالجن موجوداً منذ بداية العالم، وسنبقى موجودين دائماً. ومهمتنا هي خدمة أسيادنا.

— خدمتي أنا؟ متعجباً علاء الدين، ولم يكن يصدق ما قد سمع، كيف يمكنك أن تخدمني؟

من ثم، قال الجني: بإمكاني أن أحقق لك ثلاث أمنيات، ولكن لا يجب أن تكون هذه الأمنيات كبيرة ومهمة جداً، لأنني ليس من الدرجة الأولى.

— ماذا تعني بأنك جني ليس من الدرجة الأولى؟

— هذا سهل جداً. تماماً مثل فرق كرة القدم، هناك فرق من الدرجة الأولى والثانية والثالثة....، وعالم الجن يسير بنفس الطريقة، هناك جان من درجات مختلفة، ومن خلال أمنيات أسيادنا، فإنه وفي حال أن الأمنيات كانت أو تكون لتحقيق شيء مهم لرفاهية العالم، فإن درجة الجن ستعلوا.

— ومن الذي يقرر ذلك؟

— مجلس الأعيان للجان.

وكلما سمع علاء الدين أكثر، كانت دهشته تزداد. لا، لا يمكن أن يكون كل هذا صحيحاً. ولكن، وفي حال أنه كان صحيحاً؟ فإن أفضل طريقة كانت لمعرفة ذلك، أن يثبت له الجني من خلال تحقيق شيئاً ما.

— إذا طلبت منك أن تحقق لي شيئاً، فهل ستحققه لي؟

— إذا كان شيئاً صغيراً... نعم.

— صغيراً، إلى أي حد؟

— حسناً...، سأقول لك بعض الأشياء والتي لا يمكنك أن

تطلبها، وهكذا ستفهم الذي أعنيه. مثلاً، ليس لدي السلطة على حياة وموت الأفراد، ولا أستطيع أن أنقلك إلى موقع آخر، ولا أستطيع أن أجعلك من الأغنياء ولا أن أخفي قاتلا أو منع الحرب...

فجلس علاء الدين ليفكر وسأل الجني:

– إذاً، ما الذي يمكنك أن تحققه؟

أجابه الجني: بإمكاني أن أمنحك العديد الأشياء، على شرط ألا تكون أشياءً غير عادية. ونصح الجني علاء الدين أن يفكر في حياته اليومية، والأشياء التي يقوم بها، والأشياء التي تقوم بعملها والدته والأصدقاء... ومن ثم، إتضحت الأمور لعلاء الدين، وكان عنده طلب.

– هل بإمكاني أن آكل سمكة مثل هؤلاء الناس الذين يأكلون هناك؟ سأل وهو يشير إلى مطعم قريب.

– طبعاً!

ولم ينتهي علاء الدين من لفظ تلك الكلمات، حتى أنه وجد أمامه طبق وفيه سمكة شبوط كبيرة ومشوية، مقسومة إلى نصفين ومجهزة بالملح والتوابل، وكانت رائحتها شهية جداً.

– يا إلهي، صارخاً، ومن دون إنتظار بدأ في أكل السمكة.

فرك علاء الدين عينيه، وقرص خديه، ليتأكد من أنه كان
مستيقظاً وأنه لا يحلم، وشاهد بدهشة الجني، الذي ظل جالساً
أمامه.

وبعد مرور وقت قصير وهو يأكل، وفي حين كان حذراً لكي لا يحرق أصابعه، تنفس بعمق وفكر أن يأخذ النصف الآخر من السمكة إلى والدته. وفي الواقع، كانت معدته قد إمتلأت. رفع رأسه ونظر إلى الجني؛ الذي إبتسم راضياً إلى جانبه.

— وإذا طلبت منك شيئاً آخر، هل تستطيع أن تلبيه لي؟ من ثم شرح له الجني كيفية عمل القوانين العامة للأمنيات. يمكنه أن يطلب ثلاثة أمنيات، كما كان الحال دائما.

— أو أنك لم تقرأ أبداً أي من الحكايات؟ منتقداً إياه.

وبالإمكان طلب الأمنيات الثلاث في الوقت ذاته، أو واحدة تلو الأخرى. ومع ذلك، فإن منح الأمنيات لا يكون بشكل دائم أو في أي وقت، في قول آخر، في حال أن تطلب الأمنيات الثلاث، فإنه لا يمكنك أن تطلب أي شيئاً آخر إلا بعد مرور ثلاثة أشهر على ذلك. فعلي ان أستجمع قواي وأعيد شحن البطاريات.

كان علاء الدين صبياً حذراً، وفضل أن يفكر جيداً في أمنياته الأثنتين التاليتين. وقال علاء الدين أنه ليس بحاجة إلى شيء آخر في الوقت الراهن، وطلب من الجني أن يعود إلى المصباح، وتوجه الصبي مسرعاً إلى منزله مع هذا الشيء الثمين، حاملا إياه مع نصف السمكة الآخر. وعندما وصل إلى

المنزل ورأت والدته السمكة وكانت لا تزال ساخنة، سرّت بها كثيراً. وقال علاء الدين لوالدته، أن أحد المطاعم أعطاه هذه السمكة، فصدقته الأم الطيبة. فلم يشأ أن يخبرها بقصة المصباح، وفضل أن يبقيه سراً.

في تلك الليلة، لم يكن علاء الدين قادراً على النوم جيداً. وفي اليوم التالي، في المدرسة، قص علاء الدين سره على أفضل صديق لديه "جميل"؛ جميل الذي كان قد رأى أخاه الأكبر وهو يموت؛ عندما إنفجرت قنبلة بجانب الطريق أثناء عودته من المدرسة، والأخ الثاني، الذي كان قد ذهب للعب كرة القدم مع أصدقائه، ولم يعد من بعدها إلى المنزل. وكانت والدته مريضة. لأنها لم تكن تأكل إلا القليل، لتترك الطعام لجميل وأخاه الأصغر ليأكلوا. ومن ثم أصيبت والدته بالانفلونزا وأصبحت مريضة جداً. ولذلك سأل جميل علاء الدين:

— هل تعتقد أن بإمكان الجني الحصول على بعض الدواء لوالدتي؟

على الفور قال: إن هذا سبباً وجيهاً ليطلب أمنيته الثانية. وبعد الإنتهاء من المدرسة، ذهب علاء الدين وصديقه إلى منطقة خالية بجانب النهر، وفرك علاء الدين المصباح وخرج الجني مرة أخرى، ومن ثم طلب علاء الدين من الجني أن يحضر له

مضادات حيوية لوالدة جميل.

– يا إلهي، مضادات حيوية، مضادات حيوية، محتجاً الجني. تعتقدون أنه من السهل الحصول على هذا الدواء! فأنا لا استطيع أن أصنع من لا شيء، شاحنة مليئة بالمضادات الحيوية. فهذه مواد شحيحة، حتى بالنسبة للجان.

– فكم يمكنك أن تجلب لنا؟ متوسلاً إياه جميل.

– كحد أقصى لأمنية واحدة، بإمكاني أن أجلب خمسة صناديق.

فنظر كل منهما إلى الآخر فرحين، وقال علاء الدين كلمة واحدة:

– موافق!

وفي الحال، وعلى إحدى الصخور، ظهرت خمس صناديق كبيرة من المضادات الحيوية، فأخذها جميل بسرعة، وضم علاء الدين إلى صدره، ومن ثم ذهب مسرعاً إلى منزله.

والأمنية الثالثة لعلاء الدين، كانت عبارة عن ماكينة خياطة لوالدته. وكان يعلم أنه لا يسطيع أن يطلب أي شيء آخر إلا بعد مرور ثلاثة أشهر. وبهذه الماكينة إستطاعت والدته العمل بشكل أفضل وبسرعة أكبر. ولكن الخبر السار كان، أن والدة جميل قد شفيت بعد إستخدامها للدواء.

وبعد مرور ثلاثة أشهر، عاد علاء الدين بطلب أشياءً أخرى؛ ضمن حدود قدرات الجني طبعاً، فكان يطلب أشياء بسيطة للغاية مثل: صندوق من الفاكهة، ملابس أو المزيد من الأدوية لبعض الجيران المرضى والمحتاجين، خزانات صغيرة من البنزين التي كان يبيعها على أشارات المرور...

وكانت تمر الأيام والشهور، محفوفة بالمخاطر أثناء النزول إلى الشارع؛ ففي كل ركن وزاوية، السوق أو المسجد أو حتى أمام المدرسة، كان من الممكن أن تنفجر إحدى القنابل. ففي بغداد، كان يجهل الناس كلمة "غداً"؛ ولذلك عاشوا أيامهم لحظة بلحظة.

قال الأمريكيين أنهم غزوا البلاد للإطاحة بالديكتاتور، لكنهم لم يغادروا من بعد ذلك، وإحتلوا البلاد، وقاموا بإجراء الإنتخابات لفرض سيطرة الحكومة، ولكن العنف على أرض الواقع لم يتوقف. وكأن أتباع بن لادن إغتنموا الفرصة لوضع قنابل في كل مكان! وبدلاً من أن تتحسن الأمور، أصبح كل شيء أسوأ من ذي قبل، وبصرف النظر عن القوات الأجنبية، كان هناك الجيش العراقي، وبالإضافة إلى ذلك، الميليشيات التي لا يُعرف من أين قد جاءت، اللذين خطفوا وقتلوا الناس. وشهد علاء الدين، العديد من أصدقائه اللذين تيتموا بسبب

وفاة أو إختفاء أسرهم؛ ولأنهم لا يملكون شيئاً ليعتاشوا منه من بعد رحيل الآباء والامهات، سقطوا في أيدي العصابات والمجرمين، اللذين قاموا بإستغلالهم والاعتداء عليهم. وفي إحدى الليالي، إلتقى علاء الدين بجارة يتيمة في سنه، وكانت تنشم الغراء بالقرب من إشارة المرور، فشفق عليها كثيراً. ولذلك، فإن الطلب التالي لعلاء الدين كان لمساعدة تلك الطفلة.

في المدرسة، وفي فصل علاء الدين، كان هناك عشرون طالب، أحياناً لم يكن يحضر سوى إثنين أو ثلاثة من الطلبة. وفي أحد الأيام، وبعد أن خرج علاء الدين من المدرسة، رأى سيارة تتوقف، وخرج منها أربعة رجال، وقاموا بخطف طفلة، خديجة؛ كانت تبلغ عشر سنوات فقط، وكان على والديها بيع المنزل والسيارة لدفع الفدية ليستردوها من الخاطفين.

كان علاء الدين يقوم بتقديم الطلبات إلى الجني، أربع مرات في العام، وكان قد إعتاد على ذلك، فكان دائماً يفكر جيداً في الطلبات التي يريد أن يحققها له الجني... وعلى هذا الحال مرّت بضع سنوات. في بغداد، مات العديد من الأطفال، بسبب الجوع الحصار، في حين كان لا يزال الدكتاتور ينعم بالقصور، وأيضاً، بسبب الغزو والإحتلال الأمريكي

والبريطاني. ومن جهة أخرى، لم يكن علاء الدين مهتماً فيمن يحكم البلاد، أكان الحاكم طاغية مع أوسمة، أو ملكاً مع تاج، أو حتى مدني منتخب، فالوضع سيكون سيئاً كما هو الحال...

وفي أحد المرات، فكر علاء الدين أنه بحاجة إلى عطلة يذهب فيها إلى مكان ما في الغرب، لأن ذلك لم يكن عادلا.

أخيراً، وبمساعدة من الجني، تمكن علاء الدين من الدخول إلى الجامعة؛ والتي لم تعد مرموقة وذات عزّ كما كانت في الماضي. الآن، قتل المعلمين كان يومياً، وظروف الدراسة لم تكن مستقرة، ومع ذلك، فإن علاء الدين إجتهد ودرس كثيراً ليصبح واحداً من أفضل طلاب القانون. وجميل أيضاً، قد أصبح شاباً، وكانت والدته بصحة جيدة، ويعود الفضل للدواء الذي كان يحضره الجني. وفي الوقت ذاته، كان جميل يعمل في مكاتب الثكنات العسكرية، بالقرب من مطار بغداد، فمن المؤكد أنه لم يكن يحب هذا العمل كثيراً، ولكن دراسته لم تسر على ما يرام، كما هو الحال لعلاء الدين، ولذلك كان عليه قبول أول فرصة عمل سنحت له. وبعد مدّة من الزمن، إستقال جميل من الوظيفة، وقال لعلاء الدين: على الأقل، أنا كنت محظوظاً، فهناك كثير من الناس العاطلين عن العمل، وكان قد تحدث كثيراً في هذا الشأن مع علاء الدين قبل أن يتخذ قراره.

والدته، وبهذه الماكينة تمكنت من العمل بشكل أفضل وبسرعة أكبر.

لكنه لم يكن يرى الأمور بوضوح، ولكنه إعترف بأن المعيشة كانت صعبة للغاية في ذلك الوقت، وكان عليه العمل في أي شيء. فبعض من معارفه إتهموه بالخيانة والتعاون مع المُحتل، ولكنه أجابهم: أنه إذا كان هؤلاء الناس هم أصحاب كل شيء!، فإن العمل في أي مكان سيؤدي إلى النتيجة ذاتها. وبطريقة أو بأخرى، فإنه يجب علينا كسب لقمة العيش، أليس كذلك؟.

وعلى الرغم من أن الثكنة العسكرية كانت تعج بالقوات العراقية، وكان هناك كتيبة واحدة من الجنود الامريكيين، الذين وفي واقع الأمر، كانوا يديرون كل شيء كما يشاؤون. في بعض الأحيان، كان علاء الدين يذهب إلى مكان عمل صديقه جميل، ليصطحبه إلى ضفاف نهر دجلة، كما كانا يفعلان عندما كانوا صغار السن. في أحد الأيام، عندما كان علاء الدين ينتظر صديقه؛ بعيداً قليلاً عن المدخل، رأى سيارة جيب تخرج ويقودها أحد الجنود الأمريكيين. وتوقفت السيارة للحظة، للإلتفاف إلى الطريق الرئيسي، وحينها تمكن علاء الدين أن يرى بشكل أفضل: فقد كانت فتاة شابة، مستديرة الوجه، ولون بشرتها غامقة بعض الشيء، وعيناها كبيرتان جداً. ولاحظت الفتاة أن أحداً كان ينظر إليها، فنظرت إليه

أيضاً. ومن ثم، وبدلاً من أن تنظر إليه بنظرات العدو الجافة والمتعجرفة، نظرت إلى علاء الدين بنظرات ناعمة وجميلة، والتي أسرت قلبه. وأذهلت هذه النظرات علاء الدين، وعندما خرج صديقه، لم يتوقف علاء الدين عن طرح الأسئلة: "من هي؟، ما هو إسمها؟، وبماذا تعمل؟، هل تخرج من هنا كل يوم؟، في أي وقت؟".

– الكثير من الأسئلة التي ليس لها إجابة! قال له جميل أنه لا يعرف أي شيء عن هذه الفتاة.

ومنذ ذلك اليوم، لم يستطع علاء الدين أن يتوقف عن التفكير بتلك الفتاة. وفي أحد الأيام، في الفصل الجامعي، إعترف لأحد زملائه بأنه يحب... زميله غاضباً:

– ماذا!!! تحب فتاة أمريكية؟ كيف إستطعت أن تفعل شيئاً كهذا؟ إنهم مجرمين من دون قلب ولا رحمة؛ هل نسيت الذي فعلوه بآبائنا وأصدقائنا؟

كان ينتمي ذلك الشاب إلى المقاومة، واعتقد علاء الدين أن زميله كان على حق، ولكن علاء الدين لم يستطع أن يتوقف عن التفكير بالفتاة الأمريكية. كان قد أحبها بجنون. وكان يقول: من المؤكد أن يكون هناك بعض الأمريكيين الطيبين.

وأصبح جميل "إله الحب" لعلاء الدين، فقدم إليه المعلومات

التي أراد. فكانت تدعى تلك الفتاة سوزان، وهي من أصول إسبانية، كانت يتيمة، وهاجرت من المكسيك لتعيش في الولايات المتحدة، ولم تكن متزوجة.

– وماذا أيضاً؟ أخبرني المزيد عنها، فكل شيء كان يبدو قليلاً لعلاء الدين. – ما رأيك، سأكتب لها رسالة، فهل يمكنك أن توصلها إليها؟

وهكذا فعل، وفي مقدمة الرسالة، بعض الأبيات من قصيدة "أنشودة المطر" للشاعر السياب، مترجمة إلى اللغة الإنكليزية. وبينما كان ينتظر رداً، بدا إليه وأن العالم قد توقف، وأن الساعات أصبحت أطول من السنين، فكان يأكل قليلاً وأهمل الدراسة. وكأن الحب قد سيطر على كل جوارحه! ومرت الأيام ولكن لم يصله أي رد من محبوبته. ولذلك، إستدعى جني المصباح، وطلب منه أن يفعل أي شيء ممكن.

– ماذا؟ هل تعتقد أنني وكيل زواج؟ مجيباً إياه الجني، وكان غاضباً من طلبه هذا.

– ولكن، بمقدورك أن تفعل شيئاً لها لكي لا تتجاهلني.

– سأقدم لك نصيحة فقط. أن تصر على الشعر وقصائد الحب، لأن النساء تحب الغزل، حتى إن كانوا جنوداً.

وأتبع علاء الدين نصيحة الجني، وبعد مرور ثمانية أيام

ولياليها الطوال، وفي كل يوم كان يبعث إليها بقصيدة، ومن دون أي رد، خرج جميل من العمل مسروراً، وتاركاً إبتسامة عريضة على وجهه.

— اليوم سألتي من تكون أنت، ومن أين تعرفها، وبماذا تعمل، وسألتني عن علاقتي بك أيضاً.

— وماذا قلت لها؟؟

— لقد رفعت من شأنك إلى السماء.

كان علاء الدين مبتهجاً. فتحدث جميل مع سوزان بخصوص علاء الدين، وقال إنها كانت مهتمة بأمره.

— ومن ثم، سألتها فيما إذا كانت تريد أن تكتب لك شيئاً، وأجابتني، بأنها ستفكر في الأمر، وربما ستفعل.

وفي موجة من السعادة، قبَّلَ علاء الدين صديقه سعيداً بالذي حدث، وبدأ في القفز والرقص.

— أنت مجنون حقاً، فقد قالت إنها ستفكر في الأمر...

— إن هذا يكفيني، أن تفكر بي... إن هذا يملأني بالسعادة.

وبالفعل، فلم يطل كثيراً تفكير سوزان، ففي اليوم التالي، كان جميل يحمل الرد. وكان في الرسالة ذات الأسئلة التي قامت بطرحها على صديقه جميل. وعندما عاد علاء الدين إلى المنزل، بدأ بكتابة رسالة طويلة، والتي تحدث فيها عن عائلته

ودراسته وأحلامه.....

ومنذ ذلك الحين، كانوا يتراسلون من خلال جميل، ودامت هذه المراسلات مدةٌ من الزمن بين علاء الدين وسوزان، إلى أن إتفقوا أن يلتقوا في إحدى مقاهي بغداد. بحيث إختار علاء الدين مكاناً محايداً، لا يوجد فيه الكثير من الأجانب لكي لا يقوموا بمضايقتهم، وليس مليء بالعراقيين فقط، لأنهم سينظرون بسوء إلى سوزان.

كان علاء الدين متوتراً جداً، حتى أنه كان في المقهى نصف ساعة من الموعد؛ كان جالساً على الطاولة وأمامه كأس من الشاي ويدخن الأرجيلة. وأخيراً، جاءت سوزان، بدا إليه وكأن السماء قد انفجرت في سيمفونية رائعة من الألوان. إختفت كل الأصوات، توقفت جميع الحركات. فهناك، لم يكن هناك أحد سواهما، الإثنان معاً. كانت الفتاة قد وضعت وشاحاً حول رأسها، لكي لا يراها أحد من معارفها ولعدم لفت الانتباه. وجلست أمام علاء الدين، وللمرة الأولى كان يراها عن قرب؛ فكان لون بشرتها غامقة قليلاً، ووجهها مستدير، وعيناها الكبيرتان.. تكاد أن تتكلم.

لقد مرّ الوقت بسرعة كبيرة. هل سنلتقي مرة أخرى؟

في البداية، شعر الإثنان بقليل من الخجل. في الواقع، ومن خلال الرسائل، كانوا قد عرفوا الكثير من الأشياء عن بعضهما البعض، ولكن اللقاء كان مختلفاً جداً... وقالت له سوزان أنها كانت مترددة بالمجيء حتى اللحظة الأخيرة. وأنها لم تخبر أحداً من زملائها في الثكنة عن هذا اللقاء، لأنها كانت خائفة بأن لا يتفهموا إرادتها ويسببوا لها المشاكل. حتى أنها هي ذاتها، لم تكن متأكدة ما إذا كانت متفهمة لما يجري. وبدوره هو، أنا أيضاً، لدي بعض الزملاء، اللذين سيعترضون تماماً بأن أتحدث مع فتاة أمريكية. ومن ثم، عرض عليها الذهاب للمشي على ضفاف نهر دجلة، ووافقت على الذهاب. وبينما كانا يتمشون هناك، شعر علاء الدين بأمان أكثر، فلا أحد يستطيع أن يسمعهما، كانا ينظران إلى السماء وإلى ضفاف النهر؛ المهجورة والمليئة بالأوساخ. من ثم، بدأ علاء الدين بالحديث عن الماضي وعن أيام الطفولة، التي كان يقضيها مع أصدقائه على ضفاف النهر.

ــ في أحدى المرات، أساء إلي أنا وجميل أحد الأصدقاء، فقمنا بوضع بعض الكركم سراً في كأس الشاي خاصته. لأننا نقول عادةً من يشرب الشاب باكركرم، لن ينمو شاربه، وكما قد رأيتي، فإننا نحن العراقيين نحب كثيراً أن يكون لدينا

شارب.

إبتسمت في حان كان تستمع بإهتمام، ولكنها لم تعكس الفرحة التي توقعها علاء الدين.

– تخيل لو كان وجهك مغمور تماماً بالشعر. ضحك علاء الدين، مظهراً أسنانه البيضاء، وليظهر لها أنه إنفجر من الضحك.

ومن ثم، بدأت بالحديث عن نفسها، فهي تعمل في تلك الكتيبة منذ عشرة أشهر، وأنها كانت تشعر بالوحدة لأنها كانت الفتاة الوحيدة داخل تلك الكتيبة. وفي كثير من الأحيان كان زملائها يضايقونها، وحتى أنه وفي إحدى المناسبات، حاول أحدهم التحرش بها. وكان لديها رغبة كبيرة بالعودة إلى بلدها للعمل في شيئاً آخر.

– ولماذا تعملين كمجندة في الجيش إذاً؟

– لأنني كنت عاطلة عن العمل، وكنت بحاجة لأن أعمل في أي شيء. ولتصبح جندياً محترفاً، فإن هذا يعني أنك ستقضي نصف حياتك في الجيش. وإن معظم الأغنياء لا يخدمون ولا يعملون في الجيش. ومعظمنا هنا، ليس لدينا الكثير من المؤهلات العلمية، ولذلك إعتقدنا أنها ستكون فرصة جيدة للعمل... ولكننا أخطأنا. فيجب عليك أن تكون شخصاً مختلفاً

عن الآخرين، لتعتاد على حياة الجنود؛ وهذا لا ينطبق عليّ.

– ماذا كنتِ تعرفين عن بلدي قبل أن تاتي إلى هنا؟ سأل علاء الدين.

– جئنا، لأن هذا البلد كان محكوماً من قبل دكتاتور قاسي جداً، الذي كان متحالفاً مع بن لادن، وأنهم معاً، يريدون نشر الإرهاب في جميع أنحاء العالم.

– ولكن هذا ليس صحيحاً!! معترضاً حديثها.

ومن ثم أوضح لها علاء الدين، أن صدام حسين في الواقع، كان دكتاتوراً قاسياً، ولكنه لم يكن متحالفاً مع بن لادن، وأنهم ينتمون إلى جماعات عرقية وتيارات إسلامية مختلفة جداً. ويأتي بن لادن من المملكة العربية السعودية؛ بلد صديق للأمريكيين ومعادي للعراق، وعلى أسس ودوافع غير معروفة قد تحالفوا. وصدام حسين لم يكن يمتلك أسلحة الدمار الشامل في وقت إعلان الحرب على العراق. نعم، كان لديه بعض الأسلحة في السابق، ولكنه كان قد إبتاعها من قبل الأمريكيين عندما كانوا أصدقاء.

في الواقع، إن الهدف الوحيد لهذه الحرب هو: السيطرة على نفط العراق... وأكمل علاء الدين قائلاً: السلام؟ إن السلام لا يعني لهم شيئاً. إذا لم يكن كذلك، أنظري إلى حالنا الآن. كل

يوم هناك العشرات من القتلى في الطرقات، وإنتشرت الجرائم وازداد الإرهاب. والآن نعم، إن بن لادن يسطر على كل الميادين في العراق وفي العالم أجمع.

فسوزان لم تكن تعرف أي شيء عن ذلك، وأنها كانت داخل الثكنات العسكرية طوال الوقت، ولم تكن تخرج إلا للقيام ببعض الدوريات. أحياناً، شاهدت وسمعت أشياءً ليس لها صلة بما كان يقوله لنا الضباط؛ بأنهم جاءوا لينقذوا العراق، وأن العالم أجمع متفق على ذلك مع أمريكا، وأن العراقيين رحبوا وإستقبلوا الأمريكيين بأذرع مفتوحة... ولكن حدثت بعض الأمور التي جعلتهم يشكون في مصداقية مهمتهم، وأن هذه الشكوك قد تحولت إلى شعور بالخزي والعار.

كان الوقت قد تأخر، وكان على سوزان العودة إلى الثكنة. نظر علاء الدين إليها بحنان، وقال: "لقد مرّ الوقت بسرعة كبيرة. هل سنلتقي مرة أخرى؟

والتقوا مرّات أخرى، ومن خلال ساعي البريد الشخصي؛ جميل، هكذا كانت تلقبه سوزان، واصلوا اللقاءات، والمشي على ضفاف النهر، الذي أصبح عادةً لديهم.

ذلك اليوم، سماء تلمع فيه النجوم وضوء القمر فقط.

لا مزيد من الطائرات. لا مزيد من القنابل.

وفي كثير من الأحيان، كان الحزن على الناس الذين لقوا حتفهم في الهجمات الإرهابية، يشعرهم بالعجز عن التغيير. وسوزان كانت خائفة جداً. علاء الدين صامتاً؛ نظر إلى أعلى، وأخذ بيدها بقوة، ومعاً مشوا بصمت. وفي كثير من الأحيان، كان يمكن رؤية أعمدة الدخان المتصاعد إلى السماء، بسبب حريق ناجم عن أحد الإنفجارات.

وبعد معرفة كل منهما الآخر، جاء الإحترام، ومع الإحترام جاءت الثقة، ومع الثقة والإحترام، جاءت المحبة. وسوزان أيضاً أحبت ذلك الشاب الخجول، البسيط والذكي، والذي إكتشفت من خلاله الوجه الآخر لواقع بلده وشعبه. وبعد معرفة حقيقة الواقع، تزايد خوف سوزان، وتزايد رفضها لزملائها الجنود، الذين كانوا قليلاً ما يتحدثون في أمور خارج نطاق العمل.

في أحد الأيام، وصل نبأ إلى الثكنة العسكرية التي تعمل بها سوزان، أن مهمتهم قد إنتهت وأن عليهم مغادرة البلاد. وعندما علم بذلك علاء الدين، عرض عليها البقاء. في حين، بدا لها المشهد قاتماً في بغداد، وشعرت برعشة في جميع أنحاء جسدها؛ ولكنها أحبت علاء الدين، ومن ثم وبعد تفكير عميق، وافقت على البقاء. ففي بلدها لم يكن لديها عائلة،

ولذلك، كانت دائما تشعر بالغربة. "غُربة على غُربة، ولكن هنا، لدي رجل يحبني"، كانت تفكر. ولم تعد إلى الولايات المتحدة.

وإستضافت والدة علاء الدين سوزان، وأحبتها كما لو كانت إبنتها. ومنذ ذلك الحين، كانت طلبات علاء الدين للجني مرة كل ثلاثة أشهر، وكان يطلب علاء الدين من الجني أشياء بسيطة وضمن حدود مقدرة الجني، فلم يكن يريد أن يضايق الجني بطلبات كثيرة ومعقدة. وبهذا، كان الجني سعيداً، لأن سيده كان يطلب أشياء سهلة عليه، مثل: بعض الكتب أو بضعة أمتار من القماش أو الخيوط للحياكة... بحيث، كان الجني مقتنع أنه ومع هذا الشاب الحكيم والكريم، كان يجني الكثير من النقاط والتي من شأنها رفعه إلى درجات أعلى. وهكذا حصل، إرتقى الجني لدرجات أعلى، سواءً من خلال مساعدة الجني أو ربما مجرد نتيجة لصبر علاء الدين. أنهى علاء الدين دراسته بمؤهلات جيدة جداً. وتعلمت سوزان الحياكة على ماكنة والدة زوجها القديمة، وأصبحت ماهرة جداً في الحياكة. والمصاعب التي يواجهها البلد لم تنتهي. كان من الصعب النهوض بعد كل ذلك الدمار، لكن مساعدتهم لبعضهم البعض لم تتوقف، وكان ذلك مهماً جداً. وبفضل سوزان،

عرف علاء الدين الكثير عن تلك البلاد المسمى بأمريكا، وسوزان أيضاً، التي كانت معرفتها تزداد يوماً من بعد يوم عن بلاد ما بين النهرين. وأنجبوا صبيين وفتاة، وفي المساء كانوا يصعدون جميعاً إلى سطح المنزل لمشاهدة السماء. السماء التي تنتظر ذلك اليوم، التي تلمع فيه النجوم وضوء القمر فقط. لا مزيد من الطائرات. لا مزيد من القنابل. لا مزيد من الدماء.

وما إلى ذلك، ومن بعد جمع الكثير من النقاط، ربما سيصل الجني إلى أعلى درجة ممكنة، وذلك لخدمته طوال قرون عدة. ومع جني من الدرجة الأولى، سيتمكن علاء الدين من صنع العجائب.

النهاية